Kira and Henry

War Games

Book 4 of the Young Adult Series

Kira and Henry

War Games

Book 4 of the Young Adult Fantasy Series

By

Sandi Jerome

SmilingEagle Press

1st Edition

Published by SmilingEagle Press
A Native American imprint of SmilingEagle Productions
For information:
SmilingEagle Press
www.smilingeagle.com
ISBN 978-1-969767-13-5

Cover by: Nilesh Prabhu doggiesouz@gmail.com

Printed in the United States of America

Dedication

This book is dedicated to my fearless women warriors; Chandra, Suby, Tulaasi and Vrinda, who have made my life an adventure and my husband, Keith, who has taken the ride with me.

Kira and Henry War Games

Map of the Kingdom

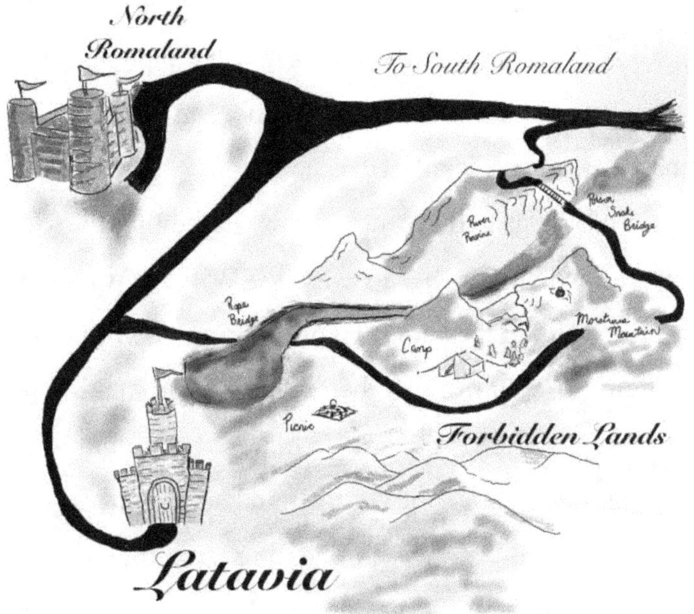

Prologue

Princess Kira hovered three hundred feet above the battlefield, wings beating against thick air with the blood moon's ancient magic. Flying was what she was born to do; what she'd hidden her entire life. Now, in her final battle, she was finally free.

Her raptor blood surged through her while below; two armies watched in stunned silence because Prince William was barely recognizable as human anymore. His body rippled with contradicting powers; phoenix fire battling ice beneath his skin, making him shimmer like a heat mirage. When he smiled, a hundred different voices echoed from his throat, all the souls he'd consumed screaming in unison.

William's smile split too wide, revealing teeth that gleamed like knives. "I've become a god, little raptor," William said, his words distorting reality around them. "I've eaten the strength of fifty soldiers, the magic of a dozen creatures, the very essence of power itself. Your wings are beautiful, but they're just meat. And I'm so very hungry."

He moved faster than physics should allow, crossing the distance between them in a blink. His hand, now tipped with claws that shouldn't exist on human fingers, slashed toward her throat.

Kira twisted in mid-air, her raptor instincts screaming warnings a heartbeat before his attack. The claws whistled past her neck, so close her feathers ruffled in the wind. She countered with her sword, but William caught the blade with his bare palm. The metal sizzled against his phoenix-enhanced flesh, and he laughed.

"You can't hurt me," he said, crushing her sword to fragments with a grip that leaked stolen power like light through cracks. "I regenerate. I adapt. I consume."

From the corner of her eye, Kira saw Henry fighting Owen's brother below them, locked in a desperate aerial duel. She saw Charles on the ground, his traditional blade somehow matching the fire-breath of his transformed opponent. She saw Peek and Aboo trying to shield transformed soldiers from arrows, their enormous bodies making them easy targets.

The blood moon pulsed, and Kira let its power surge through her veins. Seven days it had hung in the sky. Seven days of violence and transformation; of friend becoming enemy and indigenous monsters becoming... something else. Something perhaps better. Perhaps worse.

But this was the final sunrise. The last chance to prove themselves worthy or be wiped away like a failed experiment in evolution.

William lunged again, his body a weapon of too many powers, and this time Kira didn't try to dodge. She did something her mother never dared, something that terrified her more than death...

She surrendered.

Not to William. Not to fear or violence or the weight of impossible choices.

She surrendered to trust.

Kira threw away her broken sword and spread her wings wide, making herself completely vulnerable. "Henry!" she screamed, her voice cutting through the chaos of battle. "Now!"

And Henry, because he'd always understood her even when she didn't understand herself, saw what she was doing. He saw that sometimes the bravest thing a warrior could do was choose to lose. He threw down his own blade mid-strike, leaving himself defenseless before Owen's brother's descending sword.

Charles, locked in combat below, saw them both surrender. Saw the princess he'd betrayed and the squire he'd trained, choosing peace over victory. And in that moment, the old knight who'd spent his whole life proving his worth through strength finally understood:

True strength was knowing when to stop fighting.

Prince William's attack hit nothing but empty air as Kira dove past him, falling toward the ground in a controlled plummet. She landed in the exact center of the battlefield, between two armies that had spent seven days tearing each other apart.

And there, with the blood moon setting behind her and the dragon's shadow above their heads, Princess Kira did the most terrifying thing she'd ever done.

She folded her wings, knelt in the bloodied grass, and waited to see if mercy would be enough to save them all.

It had been seven days since it all began, and as she watched Henry join her, next to her, his hand grasping hers, she was ready to surrender.

Chapter 1: Broken Things

Seven days earlier... The day before the war games

Henry searched desperately through the Latavian camps. Tomorrow the war games would begin, but this afternoon he hadn't even eaten his lunch or practiced his sword play.

"Kira!" he called, pushing past soldiers who were sharpening weapons and adjusting armor. The camp buzzed with nervous energy as everyone prepared for tomorrow's mock battles against the Romalanders.

But Henry wasn't thinking about war games. He was thinking about the warning Charles had shared that morning, his voice low and urgent in the command tent. "The old texts say that treaties made under the blood moon become unbreakable. If blood is spilled in anger while the moon remains for seven days, the mock war becomes real. It cannot be stopped until one side is destroyed."

Henry had laughed it off at first. Ancient superstition. But Charles's face had been deadly serious, and now Kira was missing and his stomach was growling. He leaned against a tree and opened the wrapped package the field kitchen had prepared for him. He quickly took a bite of bread.

"Sir Henry!"

He spun to find a Romalander knight approaching at a jog, wearing the purple and silver of Prince William's guard. But the face beneath the helmet was familiar. Too familiar.

"Owen?" Henry stepped back, his hand moving to his sword. Owen had been one of the kidnappers who had taken Prince Alec three years ago. He'd been part of the team that dug up the saplings in the enchanted forest. And now, after the dangerous treaty they'd negotiated with Prince William, Owen served as the prince's Knight of War. Henry first instincts were to fight. Henry had earned his knighthood after the quest into the forbidden lands, but facing Owen still made him feel like that frightened slave boy he'd once been. He took his stance, with his hand on his sword. Ready. But then, he remembered that Owen wasn't like Prince William during the treaty signing. Owen had been the voice of reasoning.

"Wait!" Owen held up both hands, showing he carried no weapon. "I'm not here to fight. I'm here because of what Prince William told you in Romaland. Do you remember?"

Henry remembered. He remembered Prince William's smooth and mocking voice at that terrible feast, cutting through the chaos.

"The orphaned Romalander speaks. Tell me, Sir Henry, do you ever wonder about your origins? About the family you lost when Latavia's soldiers raided that camp? I've been reviewing our records, and I believe

I may have information about your bloodline. Wouldn't you like to know who you really are?" Henry heard every word in his head while he was kept in a cage by Prince William.

But Henry didn't take the bait while in Prince William's castle. He was raised Latavian. He was now a Latavian knight. His loyalties were to Latavia, King Phillip and Princess Kira. Looking at Owen, a tiny bit of curiosity boiled up to the surface.

"What about it?" Henry asked coldly. A leopard doesn't change his spots. Owen was the enemy. Yet…

Owen took a deep breath. "That's why I'm here." He stepped closer, his voice dropping to a whisper. "Henry, we're brothers."

The word hit Henry like a physical blow. Brothers? He stared at Owen's face, searching for something familiar. The shape of the jaw, maybe. The set of the eyes.

"That's impossible," Henry challenged. My parents were killed. I was their only child, spared to become a slave. A playmate for the young princess."

"Our father survived the raid. A neighbor, who had been watching me while Mother and Father were working in the fields with you, found Father. She nursed him back to health.

"But me? He never searched for his little boy, his son?"

Owen's head dropped. "Our stepmother told us that she had buried you with your mother."

"Evil," was the only word Henry could say.

"You have no idea. There is more… we have a half-brother. His name is Stanislas." Owen's expression darkened. "He isn't like us. He chose a different path."

"This is too much." Henry's hands trembled. For thirteen years, he'd been nobody. He was Romalander slave who'd earned his place through blood and bruises. He'd built his entire identity on being Latavian, on proving his loyalty to King Phillip and Kira. And now this stranger wanted to rewrite everything with a single word: *brothers*.

He wanted to take another bite of bread, to do something normal, something that didn't require him to rebuild his entire sense of self. He wanted to take another bite of the bread. His stomach was demanding to be fed. Instead, he broke off a piece and handled half of the other vegetarian items to Owen. He thought he'd refuse. Most meat eaters politely pretended they were full, but Owen took the items and took tiny bites of the unfamiliar fare, but then hungrily ate.

"I only found about this after you and Kira left the castle," Owen said between mouthfuls.

"You mean, after we escaped? To avoid being eaten?"

"Prince William would never eat a Romalander, you were never in danger, Brother" Owen said as he held out his arms for a hug.

Henry stepped back. "I need to find Kira."

"Then let me help you look," Owen suggested. Henry nodded and finished his meal. It was strange, Henry didn't have many friends and was used to eating alone. This was different. It was nice.

Later, they found Kira's tent ransacked. Her bedroll was torn, her weapons scattered, and her practice armor lay crumpled in the corner. Signs of a struggle. Henry's heart almost stopped as he knelt to examine the chaos.

"This feels familiar," he muttered, remembering three years ago when Prince Alec had been kidnapped and they'd found similar destruction. But Kira wasn't a helpless child. She was a warrior who could defeat most knights in combat. Whatever had happened here had caught her completely by surprise or it was done by someone she trusted.

"Sir Henry!"

Charles appeared at the tent's entrance, the older knight's face pale in the fading light. He glanced at Owen with barely concealed suspicion before turning to Henry.

I saw her earlier," Charles said. "Near the western ridge, heading toward the forest. I tried to follow, but I lost sight of her in the trees.

"Kira?" Henry's stomach dropped. "Are you certain?"

"I know what I saw." Charles glanced around nervously, lowering his voice. "Something's wrong, Henry. More than Kira missing. I've been noticing changes in some of our knights. Strange abilities appear overnight. One knight moved a supply wagon yesterday without touching it. Another to his horse, and the beast answered back in actual words."

Henry noticed Charles's hand slip into his cloak, closing around something. A nervous habit, perhaps. Or something else.

Before Henry could respond, two massive figures emerged from the shadows. Peek and Aboo, the twin trolls who'd helped them on previous quests. They moved with unusual stealth for creatures their size and being joined at the hip. Their mother had made special tunics for them, a new one each year. Today, they proudly wore Sir Henry's colors, when no other soldiers would.

"We saw Kira," Peek whispered, his huge eyes reflecting the torchlight.

"Like a shot bird," Aboo added, wringing his enormous hands. "She crashed. In the forest, past the boundary markers."

Henry's blood ran cold. Past the boundary markers meant Romaland territory.

"Show me," he said. "Now."

But before they could move, a horn blast shattered the evening calm. Not the friendly signal for dinner or shift change. This was the alarm, long and mournful, the sound that meant death.

They raced toward the command tent where King Phillip stood surrounded by his war council, his face grim. Queen Selina clutched his arm, and young Prince Alec, now four years old, stood beside his mother, eyes wide with fear.

"A Latavian soldier has been found dead at the border," King Phillip announced, his voice carrying across the assembled commanders. "He has Romalander arrows in his back."

Murmurs rippled through the crowd. Henry pushed forward, Charles at his side.

"Your Majesty, Princess Kira is missing. Her tent shows signs of a struggle."

The king's composure cracked for just a moment before he regained control. "How long?"

"We don't know. She was last seen hours ago."

King Phillip turned to Henry. "Take a search party. Find my daughter. The rest of you, prepare for..."

"Your Majesty!" A scout burst into the tent, breathing hard. "The Romalanders are gathering at their border camp. Prince William has arrived personally. They're demanding an explanation for the dead soldier."

"Dead soldier?" Charles frowned. "But you said a Latavian was killed."

"Yes," the scout confirmed. "But the Romalanders also found a body. One of their own men, killed with Latavian arrows."

The tent erupted in confused voices. Henry instead, formed a picture in his mind that he didn't want to see. Someone had killed soldiers from both sides, using each kingdom's weapons to frame the other. Someone wanted to start a war. Kira was missing. The Princess thirsted for war. She had training for this moment her whole life.

Charles must have reached the same conclusion. He moved quietly to Henry's side. "The arrows. Let me see them before they're presented as evidence."

They slipped out of the command tent and followed the scout who'd brought the Romalander arrows. The shafts lay on a wooden table, torchlight glinting off their metal tips. Charles picked one up, examining it closely.

"These aren't authentic Romalander arrows," he said quietly, running his finger along the fletching. "The feathers are wrong. Hawk instead of crow. And the binding is Latavian style, not Romalander." He glanced around, then slipped one arrow inside his cloak. "I need to examine these more carefully. Something is very wrong here."

Henry noticed the motion but said nothing. If Charles thought the arrows were important enough to pocket, there must be a reason. Charles had been his mentor since childhood, the only knight who trained him when no one else would train a Romalander slave. Henry trusted him completely.

Owen appeared at his elbow. "Henry. Stanislas sent me with a message. He says Prince William has brought forbidden weapons. Soul-silver blades that can permanently kill magical creatures."

" Stanislas?" Henry stared at him. "Your half-brother?"

"Our brother," Owen corrected. "He serves Prince William directly. He's trying to help us, in his own way."

Charles's eyes narrowed. "Why would a Romalander knight help Latavia?"

"Because some of us don't want war," Owen said simply. "And because family matters, even when we're on different sides."

The blood moon began to rise, bathing everything in crimson light. Henry looked up at the sky, and something ancient and terrible looked back.

Henry found Kira an hour later, stumbling out of the forest with leaves in her hair and blood on her tunic. Her eyes were wild, and she moved like someone who'd been fighting for her life.

"Kira!" He ran to her, catching her as she stumbled. "What happened? Where were you?"

"The tree mothers," she gasped. "They summoned me. Henry, the blood moon isn't just about treaties. It's a test. Every hundred years, it judges whether we deserve to continue. Those who choose peace evolve. Those who choose violence..." She shuddered. "They become the beasts they behave like."

"Someone's trying to start a war," Henry said. "Both sides found murdered soldiers with the other kingdom's arrows. But the arrows are fake."

Kira's jaw tightened. "Then we have to stop them. If blood is spilled in anger during the seven days..."

"I know. Charles told me."

"Kira, did you? I mean, you've been gone a long time… your tent…"

"What are you asking?"

"Are you trying to say? My tent looks like that because Peek and Aboo thought they saw Freddy hop in there."

"The arrows. You're an expert fletcher…"

Kira's moved her hand slowly to her sword. The anger started swelling. Her raptor wings pressed against her tunic. Henry quickly threw his arms around her.

"Breathe… I didn't mean it. It is just that you've wanted this war with Romaland for so long…" Henry explained as Kira closed her eyes and took deep breaths.

"Not anymore. Not since we were there." Kira's voice caught. "When I stood in that underground chamber and saw what William did to magical beings, when Elena showed me the children hiding in fear... I realized war isn't glory. It's just more cages, more fear, more Elena's trying to save people from monsters wearing crowns. The creatures would be the first to die. And I... I can't want that anymore."

Her voice dropped to barely a whisper. "I used to think war was about being brave. But those children in Elena's underground chamber… they were braver than any soldier. They just wanted to exist. And I was going to kill them for the glory of a battle I'd never seen." She met Henry's eyes. "I can't be that person anymore."

"There's something else." Henry hesitated. "Owen is here. He says we're brothers."

Kira pulled away from him. "Owen? The same Owen who helped kidnap Prince Alec? The same Owen who dug up the saplings in the Enchanted Forest?" She continued to take deep breaths.

"Yes."

"The same Owen who's now Prince William's Knight of War?"

"Yes."

"And you trust him?" Kira's voice rose. "Henry, you can't trust a Romalander. Not Owen. Not anyone wearing Prince William's colors."

"But he's my brother."

"He's your enemy." Kira grabbed his shoulders, forcing him to look at her. "Did you forget why he looked familiar when you first met him? He was part of the team that kidnapped Alec. You fought against him. I fought against him. And now suddenly he shows up claiming to be family on the eve of war games that could become real war?"

"Maybe people can change."

"Maybe they can't." Kira released him, stepping back. "Maybe this is exactly what Prince William wants. To get inside your head. To make you doubt yourself, doubt Latavia, doubt everything we've built together."

"You don't understand what it's like," Henry said quietly. "To have no family. No history. Nothing but a birthday I share with you because nobody knew my real one."

"I am your family," Kira said fiercely. "My father gave you a home. My kingdom made you a knight. I've stood beside you through everything. Isn't that enough?"

Henry couldn't answer. He wanted to say yes. He wanted to believe that the family he'd chosen was more important than the blood he'd been born with. He wanted Kira to say she loved him. But Owen's words echoed in his head. Brothers. Family matters.

"Fine." Kira turned away. "Trust whoever you want. But when Owen betrays you, and he will betray you, don't say I didn't warn you."

She stomped off toward her tent, leaving Henry watching her stomp off.

"That went well," he said to himself.

Later that night, Henry stood at the edge of camp, watching the red moon climb higher. Peek and Aboo found him there, the twin trolls moving with surprising quiet.

"You're sad," Peek observed.

"You and Princess fight," Aboo added.

"It's complicated."

"Family always complicated," Peek said wisely. "We shared a tunic since birth. Sometimes we want to go different directions."

"Can't," Aboo pointed out. "Stuck together."

"But we'd choose to be friends anyway." Peek placed one enormous hand on Henry's shoulder. "That's what makes us family. Not the tunic. Not the blood. The choice."

Henry looked up at them, these creatures who had been his friends since that first quest to save Prince Alec. They weren't human. They weren't Latavian or Romalander. But they had chosen him, and he had chosen them.

"What do you think of Owen?" he asked.

The trolls exchanged one of their looks.

"He smells like fear," Peek said slowly.

"Not his own fear," Aboo clarified. "Fear for others. Like he's scared of what might happen."

"And Charles?"

Another look. Longer this time.

"Charles smells like anger," Peek said carefully. "Old anger. The kind that festers."

Henry was puzzled. Charles had been nothing but loyal and helpful all day. He'd warned them about the blood moon, helped examine the fake arrows, organized the search for Kira. Why would he smell like anger?

But before he could ask more, Freddy the frog came hopping frantically across the camp. The twin trolls jumped up and down in delight.

"Freddy!" They shouted in unison.

"The forest!" Freddy croaked, his voice tight with panic. "The forest is changing! Creatures that could speak this morning can't speak now. They just growl and snap! And creatures that couldn't talk are suddenly forming words! Everything's getting mixed up!"

Henry looked at the blood moon, hanging red and swollen in the sky. The test had begun. Seven days to prove that humans were worthy to Mother Nature to exist. Seven days to prevent a war that someone desperately wanted to start.

Henry turned toward Kira's tent. They had argued, but she was right about one thing. Someone was trying to destroy them both. And whether Owen was truly his brother or just another piece in Prince William's game, Henry couldn't let old enemies tear apart the family he had chosen.

He had to find the saboteur before the blood moon witnessed something that would doom them all.

At the side of the path, King Phillip stood silhouetted against the crimson moonlight holding Queen Selina's hand. Henry bowed as he passed. The king looked older and more tired than Henry had ever seen him. He didn't want to burden King Phillip with more problems that might not even exist.

"Seven days," the king whispered to Queen Selina. "We have seven days to survive this test without destroying ourselves. Seven days to prove we deserve to exist."

Somewhere in the distance, Prince William's voice carried across the camps, smooth and cultured and menacing: "Such a tragedy, these deaths on the eve of our friendly games. But the blood moon sees all truths, doesn't it? Perhaps it will reveal which kingdom truly seeks peace and which harbors murderers in its ranks."

The blood moon rose, red and swollen in the night sky.

Seven days of judgment had begun.

Chapter 2: The Saboteur

Day One - After Midnight

Charles stood alone in his tent, the stolen arrow lay across his worktable. Outside, the blood moon hung heavy and crimson, marking the first hours of the seven-day test.

He ran his finger along the fletching again, even though he'd examined it a dozen times already. Hawk instead of crow. Latavian binding on a Romalander shaft. Someone was trying to start this war, and they were using both kingdoms' weapons to do it.

The question was: should he stop them?

War was ugly. War was brutal. Charles had fought in enough battles to know that glory existed only in songs, not in the mud and blood of actual combat. But at least in war, victory went to the skilled, the trained, the disciplined. Not to those born with wings or scales or power they'd never earned.

He thought about Kira, the girl he'd trained since childhood to be a warrior. Now she spoke only of protecting creatures, of peace, of evolution he couldn't control. He questioned Henry's Romalander brother, appearing with convenient timing and convenient information. How could Henry deny he was a Romalander? Perhaps war was exactly what they needed. One final proving ground where traditional strength still mattered. One last chance to show that steel and strategy could triumph over treaties and childhood fantasies.

Charles carefully wrapped the arrow and tucked it into his pack. Evidence. But evidence he might never share.

Not if the alternative was watching his entire world become obsolete.

Owen moved through the Romalander camp like a cat, his boots silent on the damp grass. The moon hung low and red above the tents, casting everything in shades of blood. He could hardly sleep since the delegation arrived at the war games field three days ago. Something was wrong. He could feel it in his bones, in the way the horses shifted nervously in their paddocks, in the whispers that stopped whenever he approached.

He paused beside the main water barrel and lifted the lid. The smell hit him first. Sharp. Wrong.

"Poison," he breathed.

Owen pulled a small vial from his belt and collected a sample. This was the third supply point he had found contaminated tonight. Someone was systematically poisoning both camps, and they were doing it with precision that suggested military training.

A crunching sound made him freeze. Footsteps. Heavy boots on packed earth, coming from the direction of the weapons tent.

Owen slipped into the shadows between two supply wagons and watched. Two figures emerged from the darkness, dragging something between them. No. Not something. Someone. Two someones.

The figures dumped their burdens near the fire pit and disappeared back the way they came. Owen waited until he was certain they were gone, then crept forward.

Dirk and Bart lay crumpled on the ground, their faces pale and slick with sweat. Owen pressed two fingers to Dirk's neck. Weak pulse. Shallow breathing. The same chemical smell clung to their lips.

"They've been poisoned too," Owen muttered. These two were his prime suspects for the sabotage. They had access, a motive, and the stupidity to try something this dangerous. But if they were victims rather than perpetrators...

"What have you found?"

Owen spun, his hand going to his sword. Charles stood at the edge of the firelight, his armor gleaming dully in the red moonlight. The Latavian knight's face was calm, controlled. Too controlled for a man who had just stumbled upon poisoned soldiers, even if they fought for the other side.

"Sir Charles." Owen straightened but did not remove his hand from his weapon. "These men have been poisoned. Same as the water supplies I found contaminated an hour ago."

Charles moved closer, examining the unconscious soldiers with clinical detachment. "This is troubling. The saboteur must be someone with access to both camps." He looked up, meeting Owen's eyes. "Someone who can move freely between Latavian and Romalander territory without raising suspicion."

The implication hung in the air. Owen's jaw tighten.

"Someone like me, you mean."

"I didn't say that." Charles's expression remained neutral. "But we must consider all possibilities. I propose a lockdown of both camps. Paired patrols so no one moves alone."

Owen nodded slowly. The suggestions were reasonable. Practical. But something about the way Charles had appeared, the timing of it, nagged at him.

"I will inform Prince William's commanders," Owen said. "You should alert the Latavian leadership."

"Of course." Charles turned to leave, then paused. "Be careful, Owen. In times like these, trust is a dangerous commodity."

He disappeared into the darkness, and Owen stood alone with his the poisoned men, wondering why Charles's warning had sounded more like a threat.

The forest screamed.

Owen pressed his palms against his ears, but the sound was not in the air. It was in his head, in his blood, in the marrow of his bones. Ever since he had shared that meal with Henry yesterday, something had changed inside him. He had eaten vegetables and grains instead of meat, honoring his brother's Latavian customs. A small gesture. A bridge between their worlds.

Now the forest would not stop talking to him.

He stumbled away from the camps, following the tree line until the sounds of soldiers back in the tent area faded. The trees here were old, their branches reaching toward the blood moon like grasping fingers. Owen leaned against one massive oak and tried to breathe.

The screaming softened to whispers. Pain. Fear. Warning.

"What are you trying to tell me?" he asked the darkness.

The trees did not answer in words. Instead, surged through him. Impressions flooding through him like memories that were not his own. Metal cutting into bark. Sap bleeding onto trampled ground. Small creatures fleeing as boots crushed their homes.

Someone was destroying the forest's edge. Systematically. Deliberately.

Owen pushed away from the oak and moved deeper into the woods. The whispers guided him, pulling him toward something he needed to see. The ground beneath his feet changed from grass to churned mud. The smell hit him next. Fresh sawdust and blood.

A clearing opened before him. Dozens of young trees lay felled, their stumps still weeping sap. Animal carcasses littered the ground between them. Not food animals. Magical forest creatures. The kind that could speak, that could think.

Owen fell to his knees. The forest's grief crashed over him in waves, and he understood. This was not random violence. This was a message. A provocation designed to enrage the enchanted forest, to draw its guardians into the conflict.

Someone wanted war. Not just between Latavia and Romaland, but between humans and everything else.

He had to find Henry. Had to warn him about what he had discovered. But first, he needed to survive until midnight without anyone realizing what he had become.

Henry could not shake the feeling that he was being watched.

He moved through the Latavian camp, checking on preparations for tomorrow's war games. Soldiers sharpened swords. Armorers fitted breastplates. Horses stamped and snorted in their paddocks. Everything appeared normal.

But the air was thick with danger. Heavy with something more than the blood moon's light.

"Sir Henry!"

He turned to find one of the younger soldiers running toward him, face pale with fear.

"What is it?"

"The weapons rack in the main tent. Someone loosened the supports. Three knights were injured when it collapsed. Sir Marcus has a broken arm."

Henry broke into a run. The weapons tent was chaos when he arrived. Swords and spears scattered across the ground like fallen soldiers. Knights helped their injured comrades while others shouted orders that no one followed.

Charles was already there, examining the collapsed rack with that same clinical expression Owen had described.

"Sir Charles." Henry knelt beside him. "What happened?"

"Sabotage." Charles held up a metal pin, its surface scored with deliberate cuts. "Someone weakened this. It was designed to give way under stress. Not enough to kill, but enough to maim. To weaken our fighting force before the games even begin."

"Who would do this?"

Charles's eyes flickered toward the Romalander camp visible beyond the treeline. "Who indeed."

Henry took the pin and examined it himself. The cuts were precise. Made with a small, sharp tool. The kind of tool a knight might carry in his battle kit.

"These cuts are too clean for a Romalander spy," Henry said slowly. "They use heavier blades. This was done with something fine. Something Latavian."

Charles went very still. "You are suggesting the saboteur is one of us?"

"I am suggesting we should not assume anything." Henry stood and pocketed the pin. "I will continue investigating."

"Be careful, Henry." Charles's voice was soft. Almost sad. "In times like these, looking too closely at the truth can be dangerous."

It was the same warning he had given Owen. The cold settled into his stomach.

"I will take that risk," he said and walked away before Charles could respond.

Charles checked his supplies one last time. The silk-snake threads, brought from the Romaland dungeons, coiled in their pouch like sleeping serpents. He'd watched them in action during the treaty negotiations; seen them wrap around a transformed raven, burning tighter with each struggle until the creature went limp. Deadly to raptors. Inescapable once activated. Perfect for what he needed to do.

The moon had climbed to its highest point when Owen found Henry waiting at the old stone wall that marked the boundary between camps. Neither spoke as they moved deeper into the neutral territory, putting distance between themselves and potential listeners.

"Thank you for coming," Owen said finally.

"Your message said it was urgent." Henry kept his hand near his sword. Trust did not come easily, even for brothers newly discovered. "What have you found?"

Owen told him everything. The poisoned water supplies. Dirk and Bart unconscious near the fire pit. The destroyed forest clearing with its message of deliberate cruelty. The strange new ability that let him hear the trees' pain.

Henry listened without interrupting. When Owen finished, he pulled the weakened pin from his pocket and held it up.

"Someone sabotaged our weapons rack. Three knights injured. And the cuts on this pin were made with a Latavian tool."

"So we have sabotage on both sides," Owen said. "Designed to look like each kingdom is attacking the other."

"Yes." Henry turned the pin over in his fingers. "And Charles was first on scene for your discovery and for mine. He proposed security measures that would make it easier for someone who knows patrol patterns to move undetected."

Owen's eyes widened. "You suspect Charles?"

"I suspect everyone." Henry pocketed the pin again. "But Charles has been acting strangely since we arrived. He keeps talking about maintaining traditional strength over dangerous evolution. He pocketed one of the fake arrows from the murder scene yesterday. Said he wanted to examine it, but he never showed anyone his findings."

"Kira trusts him," Owen said carefully. "He trained both of you."

"Kira trusts him," Henry agreed. "Which is why I have not shared my suspicions with her. Not yet. Not until I have proof."

"The blood moon ceremony is in four days," Owen said. "Both armies will swear their oaths then. If the saboteur succeeds in starting a war before that happens..."

"The oaths become battle cries instead of peace treaties." Henry finished the thought. "We have to find them before then."

"Agreed." Owen held out his hand. "We work together. Share what we learn. And protect each other if this goes wrong."

Henry looked at the offered hand. A Romalander's hand. His brother's hand. He thought about Kira's warnings, about the years of enmity between their peoples, about all the reasons he should refuse. But where has Kira been? He had not seen her in the camp. Sometimes you have to work with what you have.

Then he reached out and clasped Owen's forearm in the warrior's grip.

"Brothers," Henry said.

"Brothers," Owen agreed.

They parted ways at the boundary, each returning to their own camp. Henry moved through the sleeping Latavian tents, his mind churning with everything he had learned. The saboteur was not trying to help either side win. They were trying to ensure both sides destroyed each other.

"Henry!"

Peek and Aboo emerged from behind a supply wagon, their massive forms blocking out the moonlight. They wore Henry's colors still, the only soldiers who would accept a tunic.

"We were looking for you," Peek whispered. The whisper was still loud enough to wake anyone within twenty paces.

"We found something," Aboo added. "In the forest."

Henry glanced around to make sure no one was watching. "Show me."

The trolls led him to a hollow beneath an ancient oak tree. Inside, wrapped in oilcloth, was a cache of weapons. Romalander arrows. Latavian swords. The same kinds of weapons that had been used in the murders that started this crisis.

"Someone is storing weapons from both kingdoms," Henry breathed. "Switching them out to frame each side for attacks they did not commit."

"Bad person," Peek growled.

"Very bad," Aboo agreed.

Henry knelt and examined the weapons more closely. The Romalander arrows had the same wrong fletching Charles had noticed. Hawk feathers instead of crow. And the Latavian swords bore forge marks from the castle armory. Only a limited number of people would have access to these.

One of those people was Charles.

"We need to find Kira," Henry said. "She needs to know what we have discovered."

"The princess has not been in her tent," Peek said.

"We checked," Aboo confirmed. "Her tent is empty. Bedroll cold."

Henry's blood went cold. "How long?"

The trolls exchanged one of their looks. "Hours. Maybe more."

Henry broke into a run, the trolls thundering behind him. Kira's tent was exactly as they described. Empty. Cold. He should be next to her at all times, but he failed her; all because he was investigating the sabotage instead of protecting his best friend.

When he reached the tent, it had been straightened up after Peek and Aboo tore it apart looking for Freddy. It was organized, neat – Kira had been here. But a single feather lay on her pillow. Red-gold, like fire. Like a raptor's wing.

Someone had taken Kira. Someone who knew her secret.

And Henry had a terrible feeling he knew exactly who that someone was.

Later, Henry stood frozen in Kira's empty tent, his mind racing through possibilities he did not want to consider. Charles had been his mentor. His teacher. The only knight who treated him with respect when everyone else saw only a Romalander slave.

But the evidence was piling up like bodies on a battlefield.

Charles knew Kira's secret. He had covered for her transformations during training, had helped her hide her wings when they threatened to emerge. Charles could get her to quickly calm herself. He was one of the few people who could recognize a raptor feather on sight.

Charles had access to the armory. To both camps. To the patrol schedules that would let someone move undetected through the night.

Charles kept talking about traditional strength. About dangerous evolution. About what happened when the old ways were abandoned for something new.

"He's afraid," Henry whispered to himself. "He's afraid of what Kira represents. What all of us represent. The world changing into something he cannot control."

"Sir Henry?"

He spun. A young soldier stood at the tent entrance, looking nervous.

"What is it?"

"Sir Charles sent me. He requests your presence at the command tent. Says he has information about Princess Kira's whereabouts."

The words sent ice through Henry's veins. Of course, Charles knew where Kira was. Because Charles had taken her.

"Tell Sir Charles I will be there shortly," Henry said, keeping his voice steady. "I need to gather some things first."

The soldier nodded and disappeared.

Henry turned to Peek and Aboo. "Find Owen. Tell him what we discovered. Tell him to search the caves east of the war games field. Charles took Kira there during our training exercises last year. He called it his thinking place."

"You are not coming?" Peek asked.

"I am going to the command tent." Henry strapped on his sword. "I need to know what Charles is planning. And I need to buy time for you to find her."

"Be careful," Aboo said. "Charles is dangerous."

"I know." Henry looked at the raptor feather one last time, then tucked it into his tunic. "He trained me, remember? I know exactly how dangerous he is."

The trolls vanished into the night, moving with surprising stealth for creatures their size. Henry took a deep breath, steadied his nerves, and walked toward the command tent.

35

Four days remained until the ceremony. Four days to prevent a war. Four days to save Kira from whatever fate Charles had planned for her. Loneliness swept over Henry. Or was it determination?

Chapter 3: The Hunted Becomes Hunter

Day One – Later

Kira woke to pain. Her wings burned where the silk-snake threads wrapped around them, each strand searing into her feathers like a brand. She tried to move and found her arms bound behind her back, her ankles tied to something cold and hard. Stone. A cave floor.

A single torch flickered on the wall, casting dancing shadows that seemed to mock her. The air smelled of damp earth and old blood. Her head throbbed where something had struck her. A crossbow bolt. She remembered now. Flying at dusk near the western ridge when pain exploded through her shoulder and sent her crashing into the trees.

Someone had shot her from the sky.

"You're awake."

The voice came from the shadows beyond the torchlight. Familiar. Trusted. The voice of the man who had trained her since childhood, who had covered for her transformations, who had sworn to protect her secrets.

Charles stepped into the light.

"You," Kira breathed. Relief flooded through her. Charles had found her. Charles would cut these bonds and help her escape. "Thank the gods. I thought..."

She stopped. Charles was not moving to free her. He stood at the edge of the torchlight, arms crossed, watching her with an expression she had never seen on his face before. Cold. Calculating. Resolved.

"You thought what, Princess?" His voice was gentle. Almost sad. "That I was here to rescue you?"

The truth hit her like a knife to her neck.

"You did this." Kira pulled against her bonds, ignoring the fire that raced through her wings. "You shot me down. You brought me here."

"I did what was necessary." Charles moved closer, crouching to bring his face level with hers. "I've spent twenty years serving Latavia. Twenty years protecting the crown. And in all that time, I've watched the old ways crumble. I've watched tradition be abandoned for convenience. I've watched strength become something you're born with instead of something you earn."

"What are you talking about?"

"I'm talking about you, Kira." He reached out and touched one of her bound wings, his fingers tracing the edge of a feather. "I'm talking about what you represent. What you and others like you will do to everything I've spent my life building."

Charles stood and began to pace, his boots echoing against the stone floor. The torchlight made his shadow dance like a demon on the cave wall.

"Do you know what I was before I became a knight?" he asked. "A farmer's son. Seventh of nine children. No inheritance. No prospects. No future except breaking my back in someone else's fields until I died."

Kira said nothing. Her mind raced, searching for weaknesses in her bonds, angles of escape, anything she could use.

"I trained every day for ten years," Charles continued. "I learned the sword until my hands bled. I studied strategy until my eyes were so tired I could not see. I earned my knighthood through sweat and suffering and sheer determination. And now?" He laughed, but there was no humor in it. "Now a girl can be born with wings and suddenly she's more powerful than any knight who ever lived."

"That's not true," Kira said. "I trained just as hard as you did. And I'm not a girl – I am your princess, heir to…"

"You trained because you wanted to. Because it pleased you." Charles spun to face her. "You could fly away from any enemy. You could escape any trap. You have abilities I will never possess, no matter how many years I dedicate to mastering my craft. How is that fair? How is that just? How can one of you be king?"

"Life isn't fair, Charles. That's what you taught me."

"I taught you to overcome unfairness through discipline and effort. You were supposed to hide…" His voice rose. "But now I have to accept a world where some people are simply born better than others; born to rule, born to fly. That's not evolution, Kira. That's the destruction of everything that makes achievement meaningful."

Kira finally understood. Charles was not evil. He was not working for Romaland or pursuing some dark agenda. He was afraid. Terrified of becoming an obsolete knight in a world that no longer valued what he had sacrificed everything to become. He didn't hate her, he hated that she could fly.

"The blood moon," she said slowly. "You're trying to stop the evolution."

"I'm trying to save our society." Charles knelt before her again, his eyes intense. "If you and others like you participate in the war games, if you demonstrate these new abilities in front of both armies, it will legitimize this transformation. People will embrace it. They will seek it out. And within a generation, warriors like me will be museum pieces. Curiosities from a simpler time."

"So your solution is to imprison me for seven days?"

"My solution is to ensure the games proceed without evolved beings. To prove that traditional strength still matters. That skill and training and dedication can triumph over magical accidents of birth." He stood. "When the blood moon sets and both armies have competed using only their human abilities, the world will see that evolution is unnecessary. That we don't need to change what we are."

"And if you're wrong?" Kira pulled against her bonds again, feeling the silk-snake threads tighten. "If the blood moon's test requires evolution to pass?"

Charles's jaw tightened. "Then at least we will fail as humans. Not as something else."

Kira forced herself to breathe slowly. To think. Charles had trained her in survival, and the first lesson was always the same. Observe. Understand. Then act.

The silk-snake threads were tied with military precision. Charles's signature knot, the one he had taught her years ago. Impossible to untie but vulnerable to cutting. If she could find something sharp...

The cave walls were rough rock. Jagged in places. If she could work herself toward one of those edges...

"You're not working alone," she said, keeping her voice calm; as if she had accepted her fate for the next few days. "The poisoned water. The sabotaged weapons. The murdered soldiers. That's not a one-man operation."

"I work alone." Charles's voice was flat. "I always have. The sabotage was necessary to create tension between the camps. To ensure the games would be taken seriously. Real stakes produce real results."

"You poisoned your own soldiers. You could have killed them."

"The doses were carefully measured. Enough to incapacitate, not to kill." He paused. "I'm not a murderer, Kira. I tested the poison on myself months ago. The soldiers who died at the border were killed by someone else. Someone who wants this conflict to escalate beyond what I intended."

Kira filed that information away. Charles was the saboteur, but not the murderer. Someone else was working alongside him. Or against him. Using his chaos for their own purposes.

"Prince William," she said. "He's using you."

"Prince William is a monster." Charles spat the words. "He consumes creatures for power. He classifies beings by their usefulness. He represents everything wrong with the new order. But his methods created an opportunity I could exploit."

"An opportunity to destroy the very thing you swore to protect."

"I swore to protect Latavia." Charles moved toward the cave entrance. "And I will. Even if Latavia doesn't understand that protection means preserving what makes us human."

He paused at the threshold, looking back at her. "I'll bring food and water in a few hours. The silk-snake threads will keep you secure. They react to raptor physiology, burning tighter if you try to transform."

"Charles." Kira met his eyes. "Henry will find me. You know he will."

"Henry is a good knight, but soon he will be too busy to look for you." Something like regret flickered across Charles's face. "Henry is a Romalander by blood. He has family now, Owen is his brother. When Prince William's forces reveal their true intentions, Henry will have to choose. His birth kingdom and family or his adopted one. I wonder which side he'll land on. This will be a test. He won't be thinking of you."

He disappeared into the darkness, and Kira was alone with the torch and the pain. "Have I trusted the wrong person for far too long?" That was the only thought going through her mind.

Hours passed. The torch burned lower, shadows creeping closer. Kira worked at her bonds, inching toward a jagged outcropping on the cave wall, but the silk-snake threads seemed to anticipate her movements. Every time she got close to something that might cut them, they tightened, pulling her back to the center of the cave.

She was about to try again when she heard it. A whisper at the edge of her mind. Not words exactly. More like feelings translated into meaning.

"Child of sky. We see you."

Kira went still. The whisper came from below. From the roots that threaded through the cave floor, ancient and connected to something vast.

"The tree mothers," she breathed.

Francis. Ida. Mabel. She had met them in the enchanted forest years ago. Had hung upside down from their branches while they decided whether to kill her or help her. They had chosen help, in the end. But trees had long memories and longer grudges.

"The one who holds you. He cuts our children. He spills our blood. The whisper carried grief and rage in equal measure. He believes he serves the old ways. He does not understand that the old ways include us."

"Can you help me escape?"

"We cannot reach you. The cave is stone, not soil. These roots are too thin to help. But we can tell you what the blood moon truly means."

Kira listened as the tree mothers shared their ancient knowledge. The blood moon was not just about treaties between human kingdoms. It was a test. Every hundred years, the moon judged whether humanity deserved to continue sharing the world with magic.

The mothers explained that those who choose peace evolve. They become something greater. Something capable of true harmony with the world around them. Those who choose violence devolve. They become the beasts they behave like. Mindless. Savage. Eventually extinct.

"The changes you have seen in the forest creatures," the tree mothers' voice grew heavy as they explained more. "The talking animals who have lost their speech and the silent ones who have gained it; this is the judgment beginning. The moon is weighing every heart."

"What happens if we fail?"

"Then all species will begin to devolve. Not all at once. Slowly. Generation by generation. Until the memory of what you were before becomes a myth that no one believes."

Kira thought about Charles. About his fear of becoming obsolete. About his desperate attempt to preserve a world that was already changing whether he accepted it or not.

"He's going to destroy us all," she whispered. "By trying to stop evolution, he's going to trigger devolution."

The tree mothers did not answer. They did not need to.

The tree mothers' warning changed something inside Kira. Fear transformed into determination. Pain became fuel. She was not just fighting for herself anymore. She was fighting for everyone; magical and human.

The silk-snake threads burned when she transformed, but the tree mothers had given her one crucial piece of information. The threads reacted to raptor physiology. They expected her to try to become more bird-like. To increase her wingspan, to strengthen her talons, to escape through the air.

What if she went the other direction?

Kira had spent her whole life suppressing her raptor nature. Hiding her wings. Pretending to be fully human. She had become expert at making herself smaller, weaker, more contained.

Now she used that skill intentionally.

She pressed her wings flat against her back. Drew them inward. Made them smaller than they had ever been. She thought about running, swimming, jumping over fences. It was working, the human part of her was winning. The silk-snake threads, calibrated to tighten against expansion, suddenly found themselves wrapped around less mass than before.

The bonds loosened. Just a fraction. Just enough.

Kira worked one arm free. Then the other. She grabbed the torch from its holder and brought the flame to the threads around her ankles. Silk-snake fibers hissed and blackened, releasing their grip.

She was free.

Her wings ached. Her shoulder throbbed where the crossbow bolt had grazed her. Every muscle screamed from hours of confinement. But she was free, and Charles had made one fatal error.

He had underestimated the human part of her. He had focused on the raptor, ignoring who Kira was. She moved toward the cave entrance, torch held high. The passage was narrow and she recognized it now. This was Charles's thinking place. The cave where he had brought her during advanced training exercises, teaching her how to navigate underground terrain.

He had shown her every twist and turn. Every exit and dead end. Every advantage and vulnerability.

"Foolish," she whispered. "You taught me too well."

She chose the eastern passage. It led to a hidden exit behind a waterfall, one that would put her close to the war games field but far from where Charles would expect her to emerge.

Behind her, the tree mothers' roots pulsed with approval. Ahead, the blood moon's red light filtered through cracks in the stone, calling her toward whatever came next.

Kira began to run. The passages twisted like veins through the mountain. Left at the broken pillar. Right at the underground spring. Straight through the chamber where she and Henry had once practiced fighting in the dark. Charles had taught her these tunnels so well that even drugged and injured, her feet remembered the path.

The waterfall roared ahead of her. Kira pushed through the curtain of water and emerged into the night. The blood moon hung directly overhead, swollen and crimson, painting the forest in shades of rust and shadow.

She could see both camps from here. Latavian fires to the west. Romalander fires to the east, closer to the Forbidden Lands. Between them, the war games field lay empty and waiting, marked with the boundaries and obstacles that tomorrow's battles would use.

Chaos. She could sense it even from this distance. Soldiers moving in agitated patterns. Voices raised in anger and fear. Human emotions at their worst. Charles's sabotage had done its work. The camps were primed for violence.

Kira had a choice. She could slip back to the Latavian camp. Report Charles's betrayal. Let the proper authorities handle the situation through proper channels.

Or she could fly.

Flying meant revealing herself. Becoming a target, like earlier today. But the tree mothers' words echoed in her mind. Those who choose peace evolve. Those who choose violence devolve.

True peace meant accepting what you were and using it to protect others.

She had promised her mother to hide that she was a raptor, never to fly. But one afternoon, young Kira had flown anyway, just for a moment, just to feel the wind. When her mother saw Kira's flushed face and labored breathing, she thought it was fever. She'd called the palace physician, who brought with him the plague that would kill the queen within a week.

Kira had blamed herself ever since. The lie. The flying. The flush that looked like illness.

But the dragon was right. The dragons were indigenous to this land. They saw everything. The plague killed her mother. Her mother's love kept her there, tending to sick children instead of fleeing. Kira's flight was just a child's mistake, not murder.

Her mother had denied her heritage to protect everything she loved. The law was clear; being raptor banished you to the Enchanted Forest. Her mother didn't want that to happen to Kira and herself. Even the king could not prevent their exile. She would have lost the love of her life.

Kira spread her wings. Her mother would understand. Her feathers caught the moonlight, red-gold against the crimson sky. Pain lanced through her shoulder where the crossbow wound still bled, but she pushed past it. She had been suppressing this part of herself for years. She had been afraid of what she might become if she let it free.

Now she was more afraid of what would happen if she didn't.

She leaped from the cliff beside the waterfall and let the wind take her. For one terrifying moment, she fell. Then her wings caught the air and she soared, rising above the trees, above the camps, above everything she had been taught to fear.

Below her, soldiers from both armies looked up. Pointed. Shouted. Some reached for weapons. Others simply stared.

The blood moon hung directly overhead, swollen and crimson, painting the forest in shades of rust and shadow. The first night of judgment was ending. She could see both camps from here.

49

Princess Kira of Latavia flew across the blood moon's face, and the world would never see her the same way again.

She had a traitor to expose. A war to prevent. A friend to find. And this time, she would do it as herself. All of herself.

The hunted had become the hunter.

Chapter 4: Feast of the Damned

Freddy had never been so terrified in his life. The blood moon's first night was at its darkest, and deep in the forest, something terrible was happening. The little frog pressed himself flat against the damp earth, his bulging eyes fixed on the scene before him. He had followed the strange sounds through the forest, curiosity overcoming caution. Peek and Aboo were searching for Princess Kira. Henry was confronting Sir Charles. Everyone had a job except Freddy.

So he had decided to make himself useful. Scout the perimeter. Watch for threats. Do something other than hide in a pond and worry.

Now he wished he had stayed in that pond.

A hidden pavilion rose from a clearing deep in the woods, its black silk walls rippling in the night breeze. Torches burned at each corner, their flames an unnatural purple that cast no shadows. The color reminded Freddy of bruises. Of death. Of things that should not exist in the natural world.

Inside, Prince William sat at the head of a long table covered in silver platters. Robed servants moved around him like shadows given form. The smell that drifted from the pavilion made Freddy's stomach turn. Blood. Fear. Magic being twisted into something wrong.

The platters held creatures. Not cooked. Not prepared. Alive and struggling against bonds that held them to the metal.

Freddy watched as Prince William lifted a small bird from one platter. A phoenix chick, its feathers still downy and soft, flames flickering weakly along its wings. The creature chirped in terror, a sound that cut through Freddy's heart like a blade.

Prince William smiled. He opened his mouth impossibly wide, jaw unhinging like a snake's, and swallowed the creature whole.

Fire erupted behind William's eyes. His skin glowed orange for a heartbeat, veins standing out like rivers of lava beneath flesh. Then the glow faded, sinking deeper, becoming part of him. When he spoke, his voice carried an echo that had not been there before.

"The regeneration is settling nicely." William wiped his lips with a silk napkin, casual as any noble after a fine meal. "Bring me the basilisk."

Servants in black robes carried forward a cage containing a serpent with golden eyes. The basilisk was larger than Freddy, its scales glittering like coins in the purple torchlight. It hissed and thrashed, fangs dripping venom that sizzled where it hit the cage floor.

The servants wore mirrored masks that deflected the creature's deadly gaze. Smart. Freddy thought. They know what they're dealing with.

Prince William reached into the cage with bare hands. The basilisk struck instantly, fangs sinking deep into the prince's forearm. William laughed as the venom coursed through him. His veins turned black, spreading up his arm like cracks in ice. Then silver. Then fading back to normal, the phoenix fire inside him burning away the poison.

"Phoenix regeneration neutralizes basilisk venom," he explained to his servants, holding up his unmarked arm for inspection. "But the paralysis gaze remains. Watch."

He locked eyes with the serpent and smiled. The basilisk went rigid, frozen by its own power reflected back at it through whatever William had become.

Then William began to eat.

Freddy's throat convulsed with the urge to scream. He clamped his front legs over his mouth and held on with every ounce of strength his small body possessed. One sound and he would join those creatures on the platters. One sound and he would be swallowed whole, his essence absorbed into this monster wearing a prince's face.

"Your Highness." One of the robed servants approached with a scroll, bowing so low his forehead nearly touched the ground. "The preparations for the final acquisition are complete. The dragon sleeps beneath the war games field, as the ancient texts described. Tomorrow's battles will weaken the earth above its chamber."

Dragon.

Freddy's blood turned to ice water. His heart stopped beating for one terrible moment before lurching back to life.

"Excellent." Prince William rose from the table, his movements fluid in ways that human joints should not allow. He walked like water flowing, like smoke drifting, like something that had forgotten how solid bodies were supposed to work. The consumed creatures had changed him. Made him something other.

"A phoenix heart grants regeneration," William said, pacing around the table and examining the remaining creatures on their platters. "Basilisk eyes grant paralysis. But a dragon's core?" His smile stretched too wide, revealing teeth that seemed sharper than they had been moments ago. "A dragon's core grants dominion over fire itself. Immortality. Power beyond anything these petty kingdoms have ever seen."

"The beast is ancient, Your Highness," the servant said. "The texts say it was old when the first humans walked these lands. It may be too powerful even for your methods."

"All the more power to consume." William walked toward the pavilion's edge, gazing up at the blood moon. Its crimson light painted his face in shades of madness and ambition. "The war games are perfect cover. Both armies fighting above while we dig below. By the time anyone realizes what's happening, I will have eaten the heart of a god."

"And if the dragon wakes before you reach it?"

"Then I will eat it awake." William laughed, and the sound was wrong. Layered. Multiple voices speaking through one throat. "I have consumed enough power to challenge anything that walks, crawls, or flies. Soon I will have enough to challenge the blood moon itself."

Freddy had heard enough. He began to inch backward, moving with agonizing slowness to avoid detection. Leaf by leaf. Root by root. His heart pounded so loud he was certain the servants could hear it.

He had to find Henry. Had to warn someone. Had to stop this before the world ended in fire and teeth.

His back leg brushed a dry leaf.

The crackle was barely audible. A whisper of sound in a night full of whispers. But Prince William's head snapped toward the sound with inhuman speed. His eyes, now flickering between human brown and basilisk gold, scanned the darkness beyond the pavilion.

"We have a visitor." William's voice was silk over steel. "Find it. Bring it to me. I could use a small appetizer before the main course."

Freddy ran.

Henry was still in the command tent, preparing to face whatever trap Charles had set, when Freddy burst through the canvas flap. The little frog's chest heaved. His eyes were wild with terror. Mud and leaves covered his back from his desperate flight through the forest.

"Dragon," Freddy gasped. "Prince William. Eating creatures. Getting powers. Wants to eat a dragon."

Henry caught the small creature before he collapsed from exhaustion. "Slow down. Breathe. Tell me everything."

The story that spilled out was worse than anything Henry had imagined. Prince William conducting midnight rituals beneath black silk. Consuming magical creatures to absorb their abilities. A phoenix for regeneration. A basilisk for paralysis. And beneath the war games field, sleeping in darkness, a dragon whose power would make William unstoppable.

"Where is Charles?" Freddy asked when he finished, his breathing finally slowing. "He should know about this. He always knows what to do."

Henry's jaw tightened. "Charles is the reason Kira is missing. He took her. He's the saboteur we've been hunting."

Freddy's eyes went even wider, which Henry had not thought possible. "The nice knight? The one who gives me flies when no one is looking?"

"The same." Henry set Freddy down gently on a folding table. "Owen and the trolls are searching for her now. I was about to confront Charles when you arrived."

"Don't." Freddy grabbed Henry's boot with both front legs, his grip surprisingly strong. "Prince William is the bigger threat. If he gets that dragon's power, Charles won't matter. Nothing will matter. William will be unstoppable. He'll consume everything. Everyone."

Henry closed his eyes. The choice crystallized before him with terrible clarity. Kira or the kingdom. His best friend or everyone else. His heart or his duty.

But he knew what Kira would say. He knew what she would choose. She would never forgive him if he let the world burn to save her.

"We stop William first," he said. "Then we find Kira."

Owen met them at the boundary stone between camps, his face grim in the blood moon's light.

"The trolls found the cave," he reported. "But Kira was already gone. Signs of a struggle near the entrance. Burned threads on the floor, still smoking. She escaped on her own."

Relief flooded through Henry like warm water. "She's alive."

"She's free. Whether she's safe is another question entirely." Owen's expression darkened as Freddy repeated his tale of the midnight feast. With each detail, Owen's face grew more troubled. "I've heard rumors about Prince William's appetites. Whispers among the servants. Disappearances that were never explained. I never believed them. I thought they were stories meant to frighten children."

"Believe them now," Freddy said firmly. "I watched him eat a phoenix. A whole phoenix, still burning. And he's planning to do the same to something much, much bigger."

"How do we stop someone who can regenerate from any wound and paralyze with a glance?" Owen asked. "Even with both of us, even with the trolls, we can't match that kind of power."

"We don't fight him directly." Henry pulled out a rough map of the war games field he had sketched earlier while planning patrol routes. "We stop him from reaching the dragon. If the beast is sleeping beneath the field, there must be a way down. An entrance. A shaft. Something the ancients used. We find it first. We collapse it. We bury it so deep that even Prince William's new powers can't dig it out."

"That could wake the dragon," Owen warned.

"A woken dragon is better than a consumed one." Henry rolled up the map and tucked it into his belt. "At least a dragon can fight back. At least a dragon has a chance."

Peek and Aboo emerged from the darkness like mountains learning to walk. Their massive forms cast shadows that swallowed the moonlight whole.

"We heard everything," Peek said, his voice a low rumble.

"We want to help," Aboo added. "Trolls are good at digging. And collapsing. Breaking things is what we do best."

Henry looked at his strange alliance. A Romalander knight bound by blood and choice. A talking frog who had witnessed horrors no creature should see. Twin trolls who wore his colors when no one else would.

And himself, a Romalander-born Latavian who was torn between two worlds.

"Then let's move," he said. "We have until dawn to find that entrance and seal it forever."

Later, they found the entrance beneath a collapsed shrine at the edge of the war games field. The stone structure had been old before Latavia was founded, its carvings worn smooth by centuries of weather. Vines grew over everything, hiding the dark opening that led down into the earth.

Ancient stone stairs descended into darkness, carved with symbols that predated both kingdoms. The air that rose from below was warm. Dry. Alive with something vast and sleeping.

They also found Prince William's guards waiting for them.

"Did you really think I wouldn't anticipate interference?" William's voice echoed from somewhere in the darkness below, amplified by stone and shadow into something vast. "I've been planning this for years. Every contingency accounted for. Every obstacle prepared for. You are not obstacles. You are entertainment."

The guards attacked. Six Romalander knights in black armor, moving with the precision of men who had trained together for decades. Their blades gleamed purple in the moonlight, coated with something that made Freddy whimper in recognition.

Henry drew his sword and met the first strike. Steel rang against steel, sparks flying into the night. The impact numbed his arm, but he pushed through, parrying and riposting with moves Charles had drilled into him since childhood.

Owen fought beside him, their styles complementary despite never having trained together. Where Henry was direct and powerful, Owen was fluid and precise. Brothers in blood, now brothers in arms.

Peek and Aboo waded into the fight with joyful abandon. Their massive fists sent knights flying like dolls, armor crumpling under impacts that would have killed ordinary men. They were not graceful fighters. They did not need to be. They were forces of nature wrapped in a shared tunic, and nothing human could stand against them.

Freddy did what frogs do best. He screamed.

The sound that erupted from his small throat was nothing like a normal frog's call. It was the accumulated terror of everything he had witnessed, amplified by something the blood moon had awakened inside him. Raw sonic force shaped by primal fear. The scream hit the guards like a physical blow, staggering them, breaking their coordination, giving Henry and Owen the opening they needed.

"Now!" Henry shouted.

Peek and Aboo charged the stone stairs. Their combined weight crashed down on the ancient structure, cracking stones that had stood for millennia. The impact shook the earth. Dust billowed up in clouds. Again and again they jumped, each landing bringing more destruction.

The stairs began to collapse. Blocks tumbled into the darkness, followed by walls, followed by everything.

From below came a roar of pure rage. Prince William surged up from the darkness, his form flickering between human and something else. Fire blazed behind his eyes. His skin rippled with scales that appeared and vanished like fever dreams. He was beautiful and terrible, a nightmare made flesh.

"You dare?" His voice was layered now, multiple tones speaking in unison. The phoenix. The basilisk. Whatever else he had consumed. "You insignificant insects dare to interfere with my ascension?"

He raised one hand, and Henry's muscles locked in response. The basilisk gaze. He could not move, could not breathe, could not do anything but watch as William advanced with murder in his eyes.

Wings blocked the moon. Kira dove from the sky like the raptor she was born to be, talons extended, eyes blazing with fury. She hit William from behind with enough force to crack stone, breaking his concentration, shattering the paralysis that held Henry frozen.

"Miss me?" she shouted as she rolled clear of William's counterstrike.

"Kira!" Henry scrambled to his feet, lungs burning as he sucked in air. "You're alive!"

"Obviously." She landed beside him, wings still spread, magnificent and terrible in the blood moon's light. "I heard the fighting from across the field. Saw the collapse. Figured you could use some help."

Prince William rose from where Kira's attack had thrown him. Dust covered his fine clothes. A cut on his cheek sealed itself as Henry watched, phoenix fire flickering beneath the skin. His smile was wrong. Too many teeth. Too wide.

"A raptor," he breathed. "How delightful. I've never consumed one of those before. I wonder what abilities you'll grant me."

"You won't start with me." Kira drew her sword. "Henry, get the trolls. Finish collapsing those stairs. I'll keep him busy."

"I'm not leaving you alone with him."

"That's an order, Sir Henry." Her voice left no room for argument. The princess had returned. "The dragon is more important than either of us. Go."

Henry went.

He found Peek and Aboo still jumping on the collapsing stairs, Owen fighting the last of the guards, Freddy screaming encouragement from a safe distance. Together they brought down the final supports. Stone and earth cascaded into the ancient passage, sealing it beneath tons of rubble.

From somewhere far below, something roared. Not in anger. In... acknowledgment? Recognition? As if the dragon had sensed them fighting to protect it and was grateful.

The dragon was awake. But it was safe. Protected by the very earth that had cradled its slumber for millennia.

Henry turned back to help Kira, but the fight was already over. Prince William stood at the edge of the ruined shrine, his stolen powers flickering unstably beneath his skin. He had not defeated Kira. But he had not needed to. The collapse had done its work. His prize was buried beyond reach.

"You've won nothing," William said, his voice still carrying those terrible harmonics. "You've delayed me. That's all. The dragon will surface eventually. They always do. And when it does, I will be waiting."

He walked backward into the forest, his remaining guards falling in around him, and the darkness swallowed them whole.

Kira lowered her sword. Her wings folded against her back. For the first time since Henry had known her, she looked exhausted. Drained. Human.

"Charles," she said quietly. "He's the one who took me. He's the saboteur."

"I know." Henry moved to stand beside her. "But not the murderer. Someone else killed those soldiers at the border."

"William."

"Probably. To push both sides toward war. To create chaos he could exploit." Henry looked at the sealed entrance, at the rubble that stood between a monster and his prey. "We stopped him tonight. But this isn't over."

"No," Kira agreed. "It's just beginning."

Chapter 5: The Plague of Truth

Day Two – Dawn

Dawn broke over the war games field, and with it came the screaming. Kira stood at the edge of the Latavian camp, exhaustion forgotten as she watched chaos unfold before her. Soldiers stumbled from their tents, staring at hands that had grown claws overnight. Knights tore at armor that no longer fit bodies suddenly twisted into new shapes. A cook ran past her, his tongue gone, mouth working soundlessly as he tried to call for help that would never come.

The blood moon's judgment had begun in earnest.

"What's happening to them?" Henry appeared at her side, sword drawn, though there was nothing to fight. His face was pale in the early light. "This wasn't supposed to start until the seventh day. We should have had five more days."

"Until someone spilled blood in anger." Kira's voice was hollow. "The murders at the border. The sabotage. Prince William's feast. We triggered it early. The moon is judging us all now, not waiting for the seventh day."

A knight named Thomas crawled past them on all fours. His legs had fused together, scales spreading up his spine like armor made of emerald. He moved with a serpent's grace now, his arms shrinking, his jaw extending. He had been cruel to his squire, Kira remembered. Had beaten the boy for minor mistakes. Had enjoyed the power he held over someone weaker.

Now his body was becoming the serpent his soul had always been.

"The transformations aren't random," she realized, watching Thomas slither toward the treeline. "They're reflecting who people really are inside. The moon is showing us the truth about ourselves."

Henry pointed toward a cluster of tents where something beautiful was happening. A young medic named Sarah had sprouted delicate wings, smaller than Kira's but luminous with inner light. They shimmered like stained glass, casting rainbow patterns on the ground around her. She moved among the transformed soldiers, her touch calming those who panicked, her presence bringing peace to those in pain.

"She spent every battle helping the wounded," Henry said quietly. "Even enemy wounded. I saw her cross battlefield lines to bandage a Romalander once. She said all blood was the same color. That pain didn't care whose side you were on."

"And now she's becoming an angel." Kira watched as Sarah's wings caught the first rays of sunlight. "While the cruel become monsters. The blood moon isn't punishing us or rewarding us. It's revealing us."

The Romalander camp was worse.

Owen met them at the boundary stone, his face ashen, his hands trembling at his sides. He looked like a man who had not slept, had not eaten, had not stopped moving since the transformations began.

"Half my soldiers can't speak anymore," he reported, his voice rough. "Their tongues just... vanished. Disappeared overnight. The ones who spread the most lies, who reported false information to Prince William, who accused innocent people of crimes they didn't commit. They woke up silent."

"Liars lose their tongues," Kira said. It made a terrible kind of sense. "What else have you seen?"

"The greedy ones." Owen held up his hands, and Kira saw they were shaking badly. "Their fingers are turning to gold. Not golden. Actual gold. Solid metal. They can't move them anymore. Can't hold weapons. Can't feed themselves. Can't touch anything without that cold weight reminding them of what they worshiped."

"They got what they wanted," Henry said grimly. "All the gold they could ever hold."

"And the cruel?" Kira asked, though she was not sure she wanted to know.

Owen led them through the Romalander camp. Soldiers huddled in groups, some weeping, some praying to gods who seemed to have abandoned them, some simply staring at transformations they could not understand. The air smelled of fear and something else. Something animal.

In the center of the camp, a cage had been hastily constructed from tent poles and rope. Inside, something paced that had once been Lord Marcus.

The ambassador's hands had become claws. Not elegant talons like Kira's, but brutal hooks of bone and keratin, curved and cruel, designed only for tearing. His teeth had sharpened into fangs that jutted past lips pulled back in a permanent snarl. His eyes had gone yellow, pupils slitted like a predator's, holding no recognition of the humans who watched him.

He paced the cage on legs that bent the wrong way, joints reversed, forcing him into a crouch that was more beast than man. Drool dripped from his fangs. Growls rumbled in his throat. When a soldier stepped too close, he lunged at the bars with a shriek that sounded nothing like human speech.

"He can't speak anymore," Owen said flatly. "Can't reason. Can't recognize anyone. Whatever made him human is gone. Burned away. There's only hunger left. Pure, endless hunger."

"He ate people," Henry said. "At Prince William's feasts. He consumed thinking beings for pleasure. For status. For the thrill of domination. Now he's becoming the beast he always was inside."

Kira stared at the thing that had been Lord Marcus. This was the blood moon's judgment. This was what happened to those who chose cruelty over compassion, domination over cooperation. They didn't simply die. That would be too merciful. They devolved. They became less than what they had been, stripped of everything that made existence meaningful.

"Where is Prince William?" she asked, tearing her eyes away from the cage.

"Gone." Owen's voice was bitter. "He retreated to his pavilion after last night's failure at the shrine. No one has seen him since. His guards let no one approach. But I've heard sounds from inside. Screaming. Not his voice. Other voices. Many of them, all crying out at once."

The consumed creatures, Kira realized with a chill. The phoenix. The basilisk. Whatever else William had eaten over the years. They were still alive inside him, still aware, still suffering. And the blood moon was making their torment audible. Making William feel every soul he had devoured.

By midday, the Latavian camp had descended into panic.

Without Charles to coordinate defenses, without clear leadership to maintain order, fear spread faster than the transformations themselves. Soldiers who had not yet changed looked at their comrades with suspicion. Were they next? Would they wake tomorrow with scales or feathers or worse? Would they lose themselves entirely, becoming beasts like Lord Marcus?

Some turned on the transformed, driving them from the camp with stones and curses. Others tried to hide their own changes, wrapping cloths around hands that had grown claws, wearing helmets to conceal faces that were shifting into something new. A few simply ran, fleeing into the forest, preferring to face unknown dangers rather than the judgment of their own people.

Kira found King Phillip in the command tent, his face gray with exhaustion. He had not slept since her disappearance. He had not eaten since the transformations began. He looked like a man watching his kingdom crumble and knowing he could not stop the collapse.

"Father." She knelt before him. "I'm here. I'm safe."

"Kira." He pulled her into an embrace, his arms trembling. "Charles. He said... he said you were being protected. That you needed time away from the chaos. I believed him. I trusted him."

"Charles is the saboteur." Kira pulled back to meet her father's eyes. "He took me. Imprisoned me. He believes the transformations will destroy our society. He's trying to stop evolution by preventing anyone with abilities from participating in the war games."

King Phillip's expression hardened into something cold. "Where is he now?"

"I don't know. He wasn't at the cave when I escaped. He wasn't at the shrine when we stopped Prince William. He's hiding somewhere, probably planning his next move."

"We need him." The words clearly cost King Phillip something to say. His jaw tightened as he spoke them. "I despise what he's done. But he's the only one who can restore order to the camp. The soldiers trust him. They follow his commands without question. Without him, we have chaos."

"They trusted him," Kira corrected gently. "Before they knew he was the one poisoning their water and sabotaging their weapons. Before they knew he was willing to sacrifice them for his ideology. Trust dies quickly when betrayal is revealed."

"Then we need something else." King Phillip stood, squaring his shoulders with visible effort. "We need someone they can believe in. Someone who represents what we could become instead of what we're losing."

He looked at Kira. At her wings, still visible, no longer hidden beneath cloaks or bound against her back.

"You flew last night," he said quietly. "The entire camp saw you. Both camps. Word has spread to every soldier, every servant, every soul on this field. The princess of Latavia has wings. The princess of Latavia is one of the transformed."

"Yes." Kira lifted her chin. "And I'm done hiding. I'm done being afraid of what I am." She stood on the platform where war games victories were normally announced. Both armies had gathered, Latavian and Romalander alike, drawn by word that the flying princess would speak. Transformed and unchanged stood side by side, united for this moment by curiosity and fear and the desperate need for someone to make sense of what was happening to them.

Kira spread her wings.

The crowd gasped. Some recoiled, hands reaching for weapons. Others leaned forward, awe replacing terror on their faces. In the blood moon's crimson light, filtering through clouds that seemed to have taken on the same red hue, her feathers blazed like fire given form.

"I am Princess Kira of Latavia," she called out, her voice carrying across the field with strength she did not entirely feel. "Daughter of King Phillip. Heir to the throne. And I am a raptor. I was born with these wings. I have hidden them my entire life because I was afraid. Afraid of being different. Afraid of being rejected. Afraid of what my kingdom would think if they knew their future queen was not entirely human."

Silence. The kind of silence that precedes either violence or transformation. Kira could feel it pressing against her skin like a physical weight.

"I watched my mother die because I hid what I was," she continued. "I watched friends suffer because I was too afraid to use my abilities to help them. I watched this kingdom tear itself apart because I thought staying hidden was the same as staying safe."

She let the words sink in. Let them see her wings. Let them see her truth.

"The blood moon is not punishing us," she declared. "It is revealing us. Every transformation you see reflects the soul of the person wearing it. The cruel become monsters. The kind become angels. The liars lose their tongues. The generous gain the power to give more than they ever could before."

She pointed to Sarah, the medic with luminous wings, who stood near the front of the crowd. "This woman spent her life healing others. Now she can heal with a touch. Is that a curse? Or is it the reward for a life spent in service?"

She pointed to a Romalander soldier whose skin had turned bark-brown, leaves sprouting from his hair like a crown of green. "This man protected the saplings when Prince William ordered them destroyed. He risked his life to save trees he would never benefit from. Now the forest is part of him. Is that punishment? Or recognition?"

"The blood moon is not our enemy," Kira said. "It is our mirror. And I choose to look into that mirror without flinching. I choose to be what I am, openly, proudly, without shame. I choose evolution over fear."

She folded her wings and stepped down from the platform.

"The question is: what do you choose?"

The speech did not solve everything. Speeches never did. But something shifted in the camps that afternoon. Something subtle but unmistakable.

Transformed soldiers who had been hiding emerged from their tents. Those who had been driving them away began, hesitantly, to offer help instead. A knight with scales growing up his arms sat down next to Sarah the healer and asked, voice breaking, if his transformation meant he was evil.

"Were you cruel?" Sarah asked gently.

"I... I was hard. On my squire. On my soldiers. I thought toughness was the same as strength. I thought if I showed any softness, they would think me weak."

"Then perhaps the scales are armor," Sarah suggested, her voice kind. "Protection you grew because you never felt safe enough to be soft. Perhaps the moon is showing you that you needed protection, not that you deserved punishment."

The knight stared at her. Then at his scaled arms. Then he began to cry, great wracking sobs that shook his entire body. Sarah held him while Kira watched from a distance, hope kindling in her chest for the first time since the blood moon rose.

Henry found her near the supply tents as the sun began its descent toward the horizon.

"That was incredible," he said. "The speech. The wings. All of it."

"It was terrifying." Kira turned to face him. "I've never been so scared in my life. Not fighting William. Not escaping Charles. Standing up there and showing everyone what I really am? That was the hardest thing I've ever done."

"And you did it anyway."

"Someone had to." She looked at the camps, at the transformed and unchanged learning to coexist, at the fear slowly giving way to something like acceptance. "We have three days left. Three days to prove we deserve to evolve instead of devolve. Three days to stop whatever Prince William is planning. Three days to find Charles and decide what to do with him."

"And if we fail?"

Kira thought about Lord Marcus in his cage, reduced to hunger and instinct. Thought about the tongueless liars and the golden-fingered greedy. Thought about what her kingdom would become if the blood moon judged them unworthy.

"Then we become what Charles fears most," she said quietly. "Beasts wearing the shapes of men. Monsters who remember being human but can never be human again."

"Simple as that?"

Henry took her hand. "Then we don't fail."

75

"Nothing about this is simple." He squeezed her fingers. "But we've faced impossible things before. We've survived them. We've won."

"Together," Kira said.

"Always together," he added.

Two days had passed since the blood moon rose. Five days remained to prove themselves worthy.

Chapter 6: The Prodigal Knight

Day Three

Charles watched from the tree line as Princess Kira spread her wings before two armies. He had been watching for hours, hidden in shadow, witnessing the integration of transformed and unchanged that he'd tried so desperately to prevent.

He watched soldiers who had once cowered in fear now look up at her with something like hope. He watched the kingdom he had sworn to protect embrace the very thing he had tried to prevent. He watched his life's work crumble to dust.

He had failed.

The silk-snake threads still burned in his pouch, useless now. The cave where he had imprisoned her stood empty. His sabotage had created chaos, yes, but not the kind he had intended. Instead of proving that traditional strength still mattered, he had proven only that fear made fools of wise men.

Twenty years of service. Twenty years of protecting the crown. Twenty years of believing he understood what was best for Latavia. All of it ash now, scattered by a princess with wings and a courage he had never possessed.

He remembered training her as a child. Remembered the way she had gripped her first practice sword with fierce determination, her small fingers white-knuckled around the wooden hilt. Remembered telling King Phillip that she had the heart of a warrior, even at seven years old. He had shaped her into the fighter she was today. And she had used that training to escape his trap.

Charles almost laughed at the irony. Almost.

He remembered other moments too. Teaching her to read an enemy's stance. Showing her how to turn a parry into a riposte. Watching her practice the same move a hundred times until her muscles remembered it better than her mind. She had been the best student he ever trained.

And he had repaid that dedication by locking her in a cave.

"Sir Charles."

He spun, hand going to his sword. A Romalander knight stood behind him, armor dulled to avoid reflecting moonlight. Charles did not recognize the face, but something about the jawline seemed familiar. The set of the shoulders. The way the man held himself like a coiled snake waiting to strike.

"Who are you?"

"My name is Stanislas." The knight stepped closer, leaves crunching beneath his boots. "I believe you know my brothers. Owen and Henry."

Charles studied the man's face more carefully. Yes. The same set of the jaw. The same shape of the eyes. But where Owen carried himself with quiet dignity and Henry with earnest determination, this one held himself like a predator. Calculating. Dangerous. The kind of man who smiled while planning your death.

"I trained Henry," Charles said carefully. "I do not know you."

"No. You would not." Stanislas moved closer, circling Charles with the easy grace of a man used to being the most dangerous person in any room. "I am the brother who stayed in Romaland. The brother who understood that power is the only thing that matters. The brother who chose to serve Prince William rather than cling to outdated notions of honor."

Charles kept his hand on his sword. He had survived ambushes before. The poisoned snake bridge in the Forbidden Lands had nearly killed Princess Kira on her first quest. He had studied the reports of that journey. He knew how to recognize danger hiding behind friendly words.

"What do you want?"

"Prince William sent me." Stanislas stopped circling, facing Charles directly. His smile did not reach his eyes. "He has a proposition for you."

"I have no interest in propositions from monsters."

"Interesting choice of words." Stanislas tilted his head. "You imprisoned a princess. Poisoned your own soldiers. Sabotaged the kingdom you swore to protect. And you call my prince a monster?"

The words hit Charles like arrows finding gaps in armor. He had no defense against them. They were true.

"I made mistakes," he said quietly. "I was wrong about the threat."

"Were you?" Stanislas moved closer, his voice dropping to a conspiratorial whisper. "Look at what the blood moon has done to both armies. Knights becoming beasts. Soldiers losing their tongues. The greedy growing golden fingers that will never hold a sword again. Is this the evolution you want for your kingdom?"

Charles said nothing. He watched Kira fold her wings and step down from the platform where she had revealed herself. Watched transformed and unchanged soldiers begin to mingle, tentatively, fearfully, but trying nonetheless.

He remembered the feast of horrors in Prince William's castle. The way the Romalanders had expected Kira to eat trolls. The way she had refused, risking war rather than compromise her principles. She had been stronger than him even then. He had just been too blind to see it.

"Prince William can stop it," Stanislas continued. "He has discovered ancient knowledge. Ways to control the blood moon's judgment. Ways to ensure that only the worthy evolve while the rest remain human."

"And who decides who is worthy?"

"Those with the strength to make such decisions." Stanislas smiled. "Men like you and me. Men who earned our power through discipline and training. Not accidents of birth. Not magical gifts given to the undeserving."

The proposition was simple. Charles would help Prince William access the dragon through an alternate entrance, one that the collapse of the shrine had not blocked. In exchange, William would ensure that all evolved beings were eliminated from both kingdoms. Permanently.

"There is a tunnel system beneath the war games field," Stanislas explained as they walked through the forest toward the Romalander camp. The blood moon painted everything in shades of crimson and shadow. "Ancient passages that predate both kingdoms. The shrine was only one entrance. There are others."

"And you want me to lead Prince William to them."

"You know these lands better than any Romalander. You have studied the old maps. You trained in these forests for twenty years." Stanislas ducked under a low branch. "Prince William believes you can find the eastern entrance. The one hidden behind the waterfall."

Charles knew exactly which entrance he meant. He had used it himself during training exercises with Kira and Henry. Had shown them how to navigate the underground passages during their advanced survival training. The memory of those days, when he had still believed in what he was doing, cut deep.

He remembered Kira's excitement when they had discovered the underground river. Her eyes had widened with wonder as the torchlight reflected off the dark water. She had wanted to explore every passage, map every cavern, understand every mystery the tunnels held.

And Henry had been right beside her, his attention to detail, his determination to learn everything Charles could teach him. He had sketched maps by torchlight, marking distances and landmarks with careful precision. Charles had been proud of them both.

When had pride turned to fear? When had protection become imprisonment?

"You want the same thing I want," Stanislas said, misreading Charles's silence. "A world where power is earned, not born. Where men like us can rise through skill and determination. Where accidents of birth do not determine destiny."

Charles listened but did not respond. Something was wrong. The words made sense, echoed his own beliefs, but the way Stanislas spoke them sounded rehearsed. Like lines from a play rather than convictions from the heart.

He thought about the twin trolls, Peek and Aboo. When Kira had first encountered them in the Forbidden Lands, they had planned to eat her and Henry. The riddle contest had saved their lives. But it was more than that. Kira had stood strong with her sword and her conviction that eating thinking beings was wrong. She had won them over through courage, not violence.

Now the trolls fought for Latavia, wearing Henry's colors. They had chosen to change. They had evolved from monsters to friends.

That was evolution too. Not wings or claws. Just the capacity to change. To grow. To become something better.

"Prince William understands," Stanislas continued. "He was born into power, yes. But he has worked to increase that power through his own efforts. He consumes creatures to grow stronger. Is that so different from you training every day to master the sword?"

"It is entirely different." Charles stopped walking. The forest around them had gone quiet. Even the insects seemed to be listening. "I trained. I practiced. I earned my skill through years of dedication. William eats living beings and steals their essence. That is not achievement. That is theft."

"Theft?" Stanislas laughed. "The strong take from the weak. That is the natural order. That is how the world has always worked."

"No." Charles shook his head slowly. "That is how Romaland works. That is how Prince William works. But that is not honor. That is not strength. That is cruelty dressed up in fine words."

Stanislas's expression changed. The mask slipped for just a moment. Underneath was not a fellow believer in traditional values. Underneath was hunger. Ambition. The willingness to do anything to climb higher.

"Does it matter?" Stanislas asked, his voice harder now. "In the end, only power matters. How you get it is irrelevant."

Charles thought about Kira. About the way she had trained harder than any knight in the kingdom despite knowing she could fly away from any danger. About the discipline she showed in hiding her wings for years, suppressing a part of herself because she feared what others would think.

She had been like her mother, Queen Kirena. Hidden wings. Secret heritage. A thousand daily compromises to protect her family. But Queen Kirena had never compromised on her fundamental values. When the plague came to the castle gates, she had stayed to care for the sick children. She had chosen principle over survival.

Charles remembered Queen Kirena's funeral. The way King Phillip had stood frozen beside the pyre, his face carved from stone. The way young Kira had watched without tears, her small hand clutching her father's, already learning to hide her pain the way she hid her wings.

And Kira had inherited that same stubborn courage. The same willingness to stand for what was right, no matter the cost.

He thought about Henry. About the Romalander slave who had worked twice as hard as any Latavian-born squire to earn his place. Who had never complained about the prejudice he faced. Who had proven himself again and again until even his critics had to acknowledge his worth.

Charles had trained him when no one else would. Had seen something in that boy. Determination. Honor. The willingness to work harder than anyone else to prove himself worthy. Henry had earned his knighthood the same way Charles had. Through blood and sweat and sacrifice.

He remembered Henry's first tournament victory. The look of disbelief on the boy's face when Charles announced he had won. The way the crowd had fallen silent, uncertain how to react to a Romalander slave defeating a Latavian noble's son.

But Kira had cheered. She had stood in the royal box and applauded until her hands were red. And slowly, hesitantly, others had joined her.

That was evolution too. Not wings or magic. Just the capacity for people to change their minds. To see past what they expected and recognize what was actually there.

And yet Henry had been the first to accept Owen as a brother, despite their kingdoms being enemies. Henry had chosen family over politics, love over fear. He had grown in ways Charles never could.

Maybe that was the real test of the blood moon. Not whether you had wings or scales or strange powers. But whether you could change. Whether you could grow. Whether you could become something better than what you started as.

Charles drew his sword.

"It matters to me."

The fight was brief but brutal. Stanislas was younger, faster, and fought with a style that mixed Romalander precision with something darker. He moved like a man who had learned to fight dirty in places where rules did not exist. Street brawls and back alley assassinations rather than tournament fields and training yards.

His blade came in low, then high, then from an angle Charles had never seen in any formal training. It was the fighting style of someone who had learned to kill for survival, not for glory. Someone who had learned that honor was a luxury the desperate could not afford.

But Charles had trained knights for twenty years. He had faced every style, countered every trick, survived every ambush. His blade met Stanislas's attacks with the certainty of long experience.

He thought about the poisoned snake bridge, how Kira had almost died there. She had watched her horse tumble into the ravine below. Henry had scolded her for not knowing her horse's name. Small moments that seemed trivial at the time but revealed who people truly were.

He thought about the monstrous mountain, where she and Henry had faced creatures that should have killed them. The tree sisters in the Enchanted Forest, Francis and Ida and Mabel, who had nearly crushed them before Kira talked her way to freedom.

She had survived all of that. She had grown stronger from all of that. And he had tried to stop her from becoming what she was always meant to be.

"You cannot win." Stanislas pressed forward, his strikes growing wilder. Desperation crept into his movements. "Prince William has already consumed too much power. The dragon will be his. And when it is, everyone who stood against him will burn."

Charles parried, riposted, and opened a cut across Stanislas's forearm. "Then I will burn standing."

The younger knight fell back, clutching his wound. Blood dripped between his fingers, black in the moonlight. His face twisted with pain and something else. Surprise. He had not expected to lose.

"You are a fool," Stanislas spat. "You sabotaged your own people. You imprisoned your princess. You betrayed everything you claimed to believe in. And now you refuse the only alliance that could give you what you want?"

"I wanted to protect my kingdom." Charles lowered his sword but did not sheathe it. "I was wrong about how to do it. But I was never wrong about what I valued. And I do not value power for its own sake. I do not value strength that comes from consuming others. I do not value victory that requires me to become the very thing I fear."

"Your brothers stood against Prince William," Charles said quietly. "Owen and Henry. They chose differently than you did. They chose honor over power. Does that mean nothing to you?"

For just a moment, something flickered across Stanislas's face. Pain. Regret. Then, Charles saw it; the boy Stanislas must have been before Romaland hardened him. Before power became the only language he understood. The same desperate determination that had driven Charles from farmer's son to knight must have driven this boy too.

They weren't so different. Just different choices, years ago, that had led them to opposite sides of this moment.

Then it was gone, replaced by cold determination.

"My brothers are fools," he said. "And soon they will be dead fools."

He turned and ran into the darkness before Charles could strike again.

Charles stood alone in the forest for a long time. The blood moon hung above him like a judge, weight pressing down on his soul. Every choice he had made. Every compromise. Every betrayal. Examined.

He thought about the boy he had been. A farmer's son, seventh of nine children, with nothing but his determination to set him apart. He had trained until his hands bled. Studied until his eyes burned. Earned his knighthood through sweat and sacrifice and sheer stubborn refusal to quit.

He remembered his first day in the knight's academy. The noble-born squires had mocked his peasant accent, his calloused hands, his rough-spun clothes. They had called him "field rat" and "mud crawler" and worse things still. But Sir Gerald had seen something in him.

"The sword does not care who your father was," Gerald had told him after a particularly brutal day of hazing. "It only cares whether your arm is strong and your heart is true. Show them what a farmer's son can do."

Charles had shown them. He had outworked every noble-born squire, outfought every privileged prince, out-thought every pampered heir. He had risen from nothing to become one of the most respected knights in the kingdom.

And somewhere along the way, he had lost sight of why he had done it.

Not for power. Not for recognition. Not for the fear of becoming obsolete. He had done it because he believed in something. Believed that ordinary people could become extraordinary through effort and dedication. Believed that hard work should be rewarded. Believed that the kingdom was worth protecting.

When had protection become imprisonment? When had belief become fear? When had the desire to preserve become the willingness to destroy?

He remembered the riddle of the twin trolls. Peek and Aboo had asked Kira and Henry: "If you can only bring one thing into battle, what would it be?" Henry had answered "a sword." But Kira had known better. The answer was nothing. Because a wise ruler does not need the sword. Violence was not the only path to victory.

Kira had learned that lesson two years ago. Charles was only learning it now.

He thought about his own first lesson from his mentor, Sir Gerald. "A knight's true strength is not in his sword arm," Gerald had said. "It is in knowing when to draw and when to sheathe. Any fool can start a fight. A wise man knows how to end one without blood."

Charles had nodded and memorized the words. But he had never truly understood them until now.

He looked up at the blood moon. It seemed to pulse in the sky, waiting for his decision.

"I was wrong," he said aloud. The words seemed strange in his mouth. He could not remember the last time he had admitted such a thing. "I was so afraid of change that I became the monster I claimed to be fighting."

The moon did not answer. It did not need to. The answer was in his own heart, if he was willing to look.

Charles sheathed his sword and began walking toward the Latavian camp.

He had crimes to answer for. A princess to beg forgiveness from. A king to face. A kingdom to try to save, if they would let him.

But first, he had a warning to deliver. Prince William had an alternate way to reach the dragon. Henry was the one who found him at the edge of the camp. Charles saw his former squire before Henry saw him. The young knight moved through the transformed and unchanged alike, checking on soldiers, offering words of encouragement, being the leader Charles had trained him to be.

He stopped to help a knight whose hands had grown scales adjust his grip on a water bucket. The scales glittered like emeralds in the moonlight, beautiful and strange. The knight looked embarrassed, but Henry spoke to him quietly, showing him how to compensate for the new shape of his fingers.

He spoke next with a soldier whose tongue had vanished, using hand signals they had developed during training to communicate. The soldier's face relaxed as he realized he could still be understood. That he was still part of the army, still valued, still human despite what the blood moon had done to him.

He paused to speak with Sarah the medic, her luminous wings glowing faintly in the moonlight as she tended to the wounded. She was explaining something about how the transformations affected healing, and Henry listened with the same focused attention he had always brought to his studies.

Pride fought with shame in Charles's chest. He had shaped this man. He had given Henry the tools to become a knight worthy of songs. And then he had betrayed everything he had taught him.

He remembered the day he had first agreed to train Henry. The other knights had refused. "He is Romalander-born," they had said. "He was a slave. He does not belong in our ranks."

But Charles had seen the determination in Henry's eyes. The same determination he had felt as a farmer's son trying to prove himself among nobles. He had taken Henry under his wing, taught him everything he knew, watched him grow from a frightened boy into a confident young knight.

"You will be better than me someday," Charles had told him after Henry won his first tournament. "You have something I lack. The ability to see people for who they are, not where they came from."

He had been proud of those words. Now they felt like a prophecy of his own failure.

Henry spotted him. His hand went to his sword.

"I come in peace." Charles held up empty hands, the universal gesture of surrender. "And with a warning."

"You kidnapped Kira." Henry's voice was cold. Colder than Charles had ever heard it. "You sabotaged our supplies. You nearly started a war."

"Yes."

"You taught me everything I know about honor. About duty. About what it means to be a knight." Henry's sword remained undrawn, but his eyes were harder than Charles had ever seen them. "Was any of it real? Or was it all just words you did not believe?"

"All of it was real." Charles met his gaze without flinching. He owed Henry that much. "I believed what I taught you. I still believe it. I was wrong about the threat, not about the values."

"That makes it worse."

"I know."

They stood in silence. Around them, the camp stirred with the sounds of soldiers preparing for whatever came next. Transformed and unchanged. Latavian and Romalander. All of them facing the same uncertain future.

"I met your brother tonight," Charles said finally. "Not Owen. The other one."

Henry's expression flickered. "Stanislas."

"He tried to recruit me for Prince William. Offered me a chance to help destroy all evolved beings in exchange for leading them to an alternate entrance to the dragon's chamber." Charles paused. "I refused."

"Why?" The question was sharp. Suspicious. Henry had every right to doubt him.

"Because I finally understood the difference between what I wanted and what I was willing to become to get it." Charles let his hands fall to his sides. "I wanted to protect the world I knew. But I was not willing to become Prince William to do it. There are lines I will not cross. Even for the things I believe in."

"You crossed lines with Kira."

"Yes. And I will spend the rest of my life regretting it." Charles's voice cracked slightly. "But imprisoning someone is not the same as consuming them. It is not the same as eating souls and stealing essence and becoming a monster that wears human skin. I hurt Kira. I betrayed her trust. But I did not destroy her. I did not try to unmake what she is."

Henry studied him for a long moment. Charles could see the conflict in his former squire's eyes. The desire to trust warring with the memory of betrayal.

"Prince William has another way to reach the dragon," Charles said. "There is an ancient tunnel system beneath the war games field. Multiple entrances. I was supposed to lead him to the one behind the waterfall. I refused. But he will find it without me. He has Stanislas searching even now."

Henry's expression did not change, but something shifted behind his eyes. "Why are you telling me this?"

"Because I was wrong." The words tasted like ash in Charles's mouth. "About evolution. About change. About what strength really means. And because if William consumes that dragon, everything I wanted to protect will burn anyway. The kingdom. The values. The people. All of it."

"You expect me to trust you?"

"No." Charles shook his head. "I expect you to use me. I know these tunnels better than anyone. I know where the entrances are, how to navigate the passages, where William's forces will be vulnerable. Let me help. And when this is over, do whatever you want with me. Execute me for treason. Exile me to the forbidden lands. I will not resist."

Henry studied him for a long moment. The blood moon cast strange shadows across both their faces. Charles waited, accepting whatever judgment would come.

"Come with me," Henry said finally. "You can explain to the king. And to Kira."

Charles followed. He did not expect forgiveness. He did not deserve it. But perhaps he could still help save the kingdom he had nearly destroyed.

Perhaps that would have to be enough.

Chapter 7: The Second Sunrise

The fifth day of the blood moon had dawned. Two days remained until final judgment.

Kira watched Charles kneel before her father's throne and felt nothing. Not anger. Not satisfaction. Just exhaustion that went bone deep.

The command tent was crowded. King Phillip sat in a makeshift throne, Queen Selina standing at his side with her hand resting protectively on his shoulder. Young Prince Alec, watched from behind his mother's skirts with wide, frightened eyes. The war council flanked the throne, their faces grim in the torchlight.

Kira remembered another time she had stood in a tent like this, watching her father make impossible decisions. She had been younger then, eager for war, hungry to prove herself. She had wanted nothing more than to crush Romaland and make them pay for every raid, every insult, every life they had stolen.

Now she just wanted the killing to stop.

She looked at Alec, remembering the first time she had held him. How small he had been. How fragile. She had sworn to protect him until he was strong enough to be a wise ruler. Old enough to take back his throne in Romaland. That promise felt harder now than it had then, but then she noticed his eyes darted between everyone in the tent. He was calculating and learning. She looked at him and nodded. It would be alright. He nodded back. He understood.

And in the center of it all, Charles knelt with his head bowed, waiting for judgment.

"You imprisoned my daughter." King Phillip's voice was ice. The kind of cold that burned. "You sabotaged my army. You nearly triggered a war that would have destroyed our kingdom."

"Yes, Your Majesty."

"The punishment for treason is death."

"Yes, Your Majesty."

"You served this kingdom for twenty years. You trained my daughter. You shaped my knights. You were trusted with secrets that could have destroyed us a hundred times over." King Phillip leaned forward. "And this is how you repay that trust?"

Charles looked up. His eyes were red, as if he had been weeping. "I believed I was protecting the kingdom, Your Majesty. I was wrong. But my intentions were not treasonous. My methods were."

"Intentions do not matter when actions cause harm."

"No, Your Majesty. They do not."

Kira thought about her mother. Queen Kirena had hidden her wings her entire life, making compromise after compromise, swallowing her pride, pretending to be something she was not. All to protect what mattered. But there had been one thing she never compromised on: her daughter.

And when the plague came to the castle gates, when Queen Kirena could have saved herself by fleeing, she stayed. She had chosen principle over survival. She had died rather than abandon the sick children who needed her care.

Kira remembered her mother's funeral. The scent of lavender that had always surrounded Queen Kirena seemed to linger in the air even as the pyre burned. Her father had stood like stone, but his hand had trembled when he held Kira's.

"She almost flew from room to room," her father had told her once, years later. "Like a fairy. There was always a light scent of lavender with her."

Charles had made the opposite choice. He had abandoned his principles to protect what he thought was important. And in doing so, he had lost everything.

Kira stepped forward. "Father."

King Phillip looked at her. The anger in his eyes softened slightly when he saw her face. "Kira. This man hurt you. He deserves justice."

"He does." Kira moved to stand beside her father's throne. Her wings rustled beneath her cloak. She no longer bothered to bind them flat. "But we have two days until the blood moon sets. Two days before Prince

William finds another way to the dragon. Two days to prove we deserve to evolve rather than devolve."

She paused, looking down at Charles. He met her eyes without flinching, but she could see the shame written in every line of his face.

"Charles knows the old tunnels," she continued. "He knows Prince William's tactics. He knows where the alternate entrances are and how to defend them. We need that knowledge."

"You would spare the man who kidnapped you?"

"I would let him earn redemption." Kira's voice was steady. "The blood moon judges us by our choices. Charles made terrible choices. But he is here now, warning us, offering to help. That is also a choice. Let him make enough good ones to balance the scales."

She remembered standing before the tree sisters in the Enchanted Forest. Francis, Ida, and Mabel had wanted to kill her and Henry for the sins of other humans. Their bark-faces had been twisted with grief and fury as they demanded to know what humans had done with their saplings.

But Kira had convinced them that she was not their enemy. She had earned their trust through honesty, not violence. She had talked her way to freedom when fighting would have meant death.

If trees could learn to trust a human, maybe a traitor could learn to be loyal again.

Queen Selina spoke for the first time. "The princess speaks wisely, my lord. We can execute Charles after the crisis has passed. Or we can use his knowledge now and decide his fate later. But if Prince William consumes that dragon, there will be no kingdom left to dispense justice."

Kira saw her stepmother's hand tighten on her father's shoulder. Queen Selina had lost her first husband to the Romalander civil war. She knew what it meant to face enemies who would stop at nothing. She knew the cost of making hard choices.

King Phillip was silent for a long moment. His eyes moved from Charles to Kira to the war council to his wife. Kira could see him weighing options, calculating risks, doing the math of survival that all rulers learned to do.

Finally, he nodded slowly.

"You will fight beside us," he told Charles. "You will help protect the dragon from Prince William. You will share everything you know about the tunnels and the defenses and the enemy's plans. And when this is over, if we survive, you will stand trial for your crimes. The outcome is not guaranteed. You may still hang."

"I accept." Charles bowed his head. "Thank you, Your Majesty. Princess."

"Do not thank me yet." Kira's voice was hard. "You have not begun to pay for what you did."

The war games began at dawn. But not the mock battles that had been planned. Real combat between real armies, with the fate of both kingdoms hanging in the balance.

Prince William had made his move overnight. Half the Romalander army had remained loyal to him, seduced by promises of power and the fear of transformation. The other half had defected, sickened by what they had witnessed at his midnight feasts. Sickened by the screams that came from his pavilion when he consumed creatures. Sickened by the way their prince had become something less than human in his pursuit of becoming something more.

Kira remembered the feast of horrors in Romaland. The silver platters with roasted trolls. Prince William's smooth and menacing voice as he explained that in his kingdom, thinking beings were meat. She had refused to eat. She had stood on principle when everyone told her to compromise.

"Such a tragedy, these deaths on the eve of our friendly games," William had said that first night, his voice smooth and cultured and menacing. "But the blood moon sees all truths, doesn't it? Perhaps it will reveal which kingdom truly seeks peace and which harbors murderers in its ranks."

Now she understood why she had been right to refuse.

Owen led the defectors into the Latavian camp just as the sun rose. Three hundred knights and soldiers, still wearing their Romalander purple but with white cloths tied around their arms to mark them as allies.

Henry ran to meet them. Kira watched the two brothers embrace, and something twisted in her chest. She had been so angry at Henry for trusting Owen. Had accused him of betraying Latavia by accepting a Romalander as family.

She remembered the argument they had that first night of the blood moon. "He's your enemy," she had told Henry. "He was part of the team that kidnapped Alec. You fought against him. I fought against him. And now suddenly he shows up claiming to be family on the eve of war games that could become real war?"

"Maybe people can change," Henry had said quietly.

"Maybe they can't," she had answered. "Maybe this is exactly what Prince William wants. To get inside your head. To make you doubt yourself, doubt Latavia, doubt everything we've built together."

Now, watching the brothers hold each other, she understood what Henry had known all along. Owen had changed. The kidnapper who had helped take Prince Alec was not the same man who now stood ready to fight against his own prince. People could evolve. They just needed the chance.

"I am your family," she had told him. "My father gave you a home. My kingdom made you a knight. I've stood beside you through everything. Isn't that enough?"

But she had been wrong. Family was not about blood or borders. It was about choice. About who you stood with when the darkness came.

"He is digging," Owen reported to the hastily assembled war council. His face was pale, his eyes haunted by things he had seen. "Using the transformed soldiers who have devolved. They dig like animals now. No tools, just claws and teeth tearing at the earth. They do not stop. They do not rest. They just dig and dig and dig."

"How long until he reaches the dragon?" King Phillip asked.

"Hours. Maybe less." Owen's face was grim. "He found the eastern entrance. The one behind the waterfall. His forces are pouring through it even as we speak."

Charles leaned forward. "There are chokepoints in those tunnels. Places where a small force could hold off a larger one. If we move now, we might be able to block his advance."

"We do not have enough soldiers to hold the tunnels and defend the camp," one of the generals objected. "If William sends forces above ground while we are underground..."

"He will not." Owen shook his head. "He does not care about the camp. He does not care about territory or victory in the traditional sense. He only cares about the dragon. Everything else is a distraction."

"What about his brother?" Henry asked. "Stanislas. He is still out there."

Owen's expression darkened. "Stanislas leads the rearguard. He will be at the tunnel entrance, making sure no one follows William underground." He paused, and Kira saw pain flash across his face. "He is dangerous, Henry. More dangerous than you know. He has spent years learning how to kill efficiently. How to exploit weaknesses. How to destroy people from the inside out."

"He is still our brother."

"Blood does not make family." Owen's voice was heavy with old pain. "Stanislas made his choice a long time ago. He chose power over everything else. There is nothing left of the brother I knew."

Kira thought about Queen Selina's first husband, King Alexander of South Romaland. He had been murdered by his own knights in the civil war. Family had killed family. Brothers had betrayed brothers. That was the Romalander way.

But it did not have to be the only way.

She spread her wings and rose slightly from the ground. "Then we do not try to save him. We stop him. We stop all of them." She looked around the tent at the faces watching her. Scared. Uncertain. But still standing. "We meet William on the field. All of us. Transformed and unchanged. Latavian and Romalander. Every being who refuses to let a monster consume the world."

"Against Prince William?" The older general who had objected before shook his head. "He has consumed too much power. We cannot defeat him in direct combat."

"Maybe not." Kira landed softly. "But we can slow him down. We can give the dragon time to fully wake. And we can show the blood moon that humanity still has the capacity for courage. For sacrifice. For choosing what is right over what is safe."

She thought about her mother's words, the ones King Phillip had shared with her years ago. "A wise ruler doesn't need the sword. But sometimes, the sword is what justice demands."

Today, she would learn which kind of ruler she was meant to be.

"The princess is right." King Phillip stood. "We fight. Not because we are certain of victory. But because some things are worth fighting for regardless of the outcome. The kingdom. Our people. The future we hope to build. These things matter more than our survival."

He drew his sword and held it high. The blade caught the light of the rising sun and the fading blood moon, gleaming silver and crimson at once.

"For Latavia!"

"For Latavia!" The cry echoed through the tent and spread to the camp beyond. Latavian and Romalander voices mingling together.

Transformed and unchanged. All of them choosing to face the darkness rather than flee from it.

Kira watched her father, this man who had raised her alone after her mother died. He had taught her to ride and to fight, but more importantly, he had taught her to think. "A wise ruler doesn't need the sword," he had told her once. "But a wise ruler must know when the sword is all that remains."

She did not understand then. She understood now.

The tent emptied as commanders rushed to their units. Queen Selina gathered Prince Alec in her arms, pressing a kiss to his forehead before handing him to a trusted guard who would take him to safety. The boy looked back at Kira with eyes too old for his young face. She held out her hand to him.

Alec reached for her hand with small fingers. "You come back, right? Kira comes back?"

His voice was so small, so certain that promises could be kept if spoken aloud.

Kira knelt before him, squeezing his hand. "I promise I will do everything in my power to come back to you, little brother. And if I do not, remember what I taught you. A wise ruler protects the weak because the strength of the kingdom is determined by its weakest subject."

Alec nodded solemnly. "I remember. I will protect you … when I am bigger."

"I know you will." Kira kissed his forehead and stood. "Now go with the guard. And no matter what you hear, no matter what happens, do not come out until someone you trust tells you it is safe."

She watched them leave, feeling the weight of responsibility settle more heavily on her shoulders. This was what it meant to be a ruler. Not just fighting battles, but carrying the hopes of everyone who depended on you.

The armies gathered on the war games field as the blood moon hung fat and crimson above them. Two days of crimson light remained. Two days to determine whether they would evolve or devolve. Two days to prove themselves worthy of continued existence.

Kira flew above her troops, her wings catching the strange red light. Below her, she could see the full scope of their alliance. Latavian knights in silver armor, their blades gleaming. Romalander defectors in purple and black, white cloths fluttering from their arms. Peek and Aboo towering above everyone, their shared tunic now bearing the colors of both kingdoms sewn together with rough stitches.

The trolls had been enemies once. They had planned to eat Kira and Henry in that cave in the Forbidden Lands. Kira remembered waking up to find them arguing about who would get to eat the "plump one." She had grabbed her sword and lunged at them, only to have it snatched away like a twig.

But then came the riddles. And the laughter. And the slow realization that these creatures, these monsters, were not so different from humans after all. They told jokes. They argued over food. They loved their home and feared the outside world.

"It's my turn," Aboo had announced that first morning, prodding at Henry. "You ate the bigger warthog last week."

"This one is mine," Peek had argued back. "It looks plump."

Now they stood ready to die for the kingdom that had accepted them. For the princess who had seen past their monstrous appearance to the souls beneath.

That was evolution. That was the blood moon's true gift. Not wings or scales or magic powers. Just the chance to become something better than what you started as.

And among them, the transformed. Soldiers with scales and feathers and stranger things, standing beside unchanged humans who had chosen to accept them. Sarah the medic with her luminous wings, ready to heal whoever needed healing regardless of which side they had started on. The knight with bark for skin, leaves sprouting from his hair, carrying a Latavian banner in one hand and a Romalander banner in the other.

Kira saw a soldier whose fingers had fused into golden claws, the blood moon's judgment on his greed. But instead of hiding in shame, he stood in the front rank, ready to use those claws to defend the kingdom he had once tried to steal from. His transformation had become his redemption.

She saw a knight whose voice had transformed into birdsong, unable to speak human words but still able to communicate through the complex trills and whistles that his companions had learned to understand. He had found a new way to be useful, his birdsong carrying commands across the battlefield faster than any shouted order.

She saw two former enemies, a Latavian and a Romalander, standing shoulder to shoulder, their old grudges forgotten in the face of a greater threat. The Latavian had lost a brother to Romalander raiders years ago. The Romalander had watched his village burn during a Latavian counter-raid. Yet here they stood, ready to die for each other.

Evolution and tradition. Change and continuity. All of them united against a common enemy.

Freddy the frog hopped from soldier to soldier, croaking encouragement in his high-pitched voice. "The forest believes in you," he told each one. "The trees are watching. The creatures are hoping. Show them that humans can be worthy of this world."

Freddy the frog sat on Henry's shoulder, his bulging eyes scanning the enemy lines across the field. "There are too many of them," the frog said quietly. "The forest says William has consumed three more creatures since yesterday. A phoenix. A basilisk. A unicorn he found wandering lost in the woods."

"There are always too many." Henry drew his sword. "We fight anyway."

Owen stood on his other side, his own blade catching the moonlight. "Brothers fight together."

"Brothers," Henry agreed. He looked at the Romalander forces across the field. Somewhere among them was Stanislas. The brother who had chosen differently. The brother who would try to kill them both before this day was done.

But Henry had made his choice. He would not let one brother's betrayal poison his love for another.

Kira descended to hover beside them. "Whatever happens, we stay together. We do not let them separate us. We do not let them turn us against each other."

"Like the tree sisters tried to do," Henry said. "When they captured us and demanded to know where their children were. They wanted us to blame each other."

"But we refused." Kira reached out and clasped his hand. "We stood together then. We stand together now."

She remembered hanging upside down from those ancient trees, Francis and Ida and Mabel's bark-faces twisted with grief. She had been completely helpless, suspended by magical vines hundreds of feet in the air. But she had not given up. She had talked. She had listened. She had found common ground with beings who had every reason to hate her.

Maybe she could do the same today. Maybe violence was not the only answer.

Across the field, Prince William emerged from his pavilion. Even from this distance, Kira could see that he was barely human anymore. His body flickered between shapes like a candle flame in wind. Fire blazed beneath his skin one moment, scales rippled across it the next. His eyes shifted colors constantly. Human brown. Basilisk gold. Phoenix orange. Something ancient and hungry that had no name.

He had consumed the phoenix three days ago. The basilisk the day after. Rumors said he had found a unicorn in the forest and devoured it last night. Each creature added to his power. Each soul screaming inside him made him stronger.

And hungrier.

When he spoke, a hundred stolen voices echoed from his throat.

"LITTLE RAPTOR. COME DOWN AND FACE ME."

Kira looked at Henry. At Owen. At the army of evolved and unchanged, Latavian and Romalander, all standing together against a monster of their own making.

She thought about her mother. About the plague that had taken her. About the choice Queen Kirena had made to stay and help instead of running to safety.

Some things were worth dying for.

Charles appeared at their side, his sword drawn. "The eastern tunnel entrance is there." He pointed toward a ridge half a mile distant. "If we can reach it before William's forces seal it, we might be able to flank him underground."

"You would lead us into the tunnels you were supposed to betray us through?" Kira asked.

"Yes." Charles met her eyes. "I know I have not earned your trust. But I know those passages better than anyone alive. Let me show you I can still be useful to this kingdom."

Kira studied him for a long moment. The man who had trained her. The man who had betrayed her. The man who was now asking for a chance to make things right.

"Fine," she said. "But Henry goes with you. And if you betray us again, he has my permission to kill you himself."

Charles nodded slowly. "I would expect nothing less, Princess."

Henry clasped Owen's arm. "Watch over her."

"I will guard her with my life," Owen promised.

"As will we!" Peek and Aboo thundered together, moving to flank Kira on either side. Their massive forms cast long shadows in the blood moon's light. "Princess is friend. Friends protect friends."

Kira felt a warmth spread through her chest. These creatures had been her enemies once. Now they were her family. The blood moon was right. Evolution was not about what you were born as. It was about what you chose to become.

The Romalander forces began their advance. Drums pounded a slow, ominous rhythm. Banners snapped in a wind that seemed to blow from everywhere and nowhere. The devolved soldiers shambled at the front, their humanity stripped away by their own cruelty. Behind them marched the loyal Romalanders, their faces grim beneath their helmets.

And at the center of it all, Prince William floated above the ground, his body wreathed in stolen fire, his eyes blazing with a dozen different colors.

"LATAVIA!" he thundered, and a hundred voices echoed from his throat. "YOU HAVE HARBORED TRAITORS AND MONSTERS! YOU HAVE DEFIED THE NATURAL ORDER! TODAY YOU WILL LEARN THE COST OF WEAKNESS!"

Kira rose higher into the air, her wings spread wide. She was not hiding anymore. She was not ashamed anymore. She was exactly what the blood moon had revealed her to be: a princess with wings and the heart of a warrior.

"WILLIAM!" she shouted back, and her voice carried across the field with a strength that surprised even her. "YOU HAVE CONSUMED INNOCENT SOULS! YOU HAVE DEVOURED CREATURES

WHOSE ONLY CRIME WAS EXISTING! TODAY YOU WILL LEARN THAT POWER STOLEN IS POWER CORRUPTED!"

The armies clashed.

Steel met steel. Transformed met unchanged. The devolved soldiers fell first, their animal instincts no match for trained warriors working together. But there were so many of them. For every one that fell, two more pressed forward.

Kira dove through the chaos, her sword singing. She had trained for this her whole life. Every lesson Charles had taught her, every technique Henry had helped her perfect, every mistake she had learned from. All of it came together now in a dance of death and survival.

She remembered Charles's voice during her first real battle. "Do not think," he had said. "Let your body remember what your mind has forgotten. Trust your training."

She trusted it now. Her sword moved before her eyes could follow, blocking strikes she had not consciously seen, finding gaps in armor she had not consciously noticed. Her wings carried her above danger, brought her down behind enemies, made her impossible to predict.

A devolved soldier lunged at her, its claws reaching for her wings. She twisted, slashed, and felt her blade bite deep. The creature fell, and she was already moving, already seeking her next opponent.

Owen fought at her left, his Romalander training blending perfectly with Latavian tactics. Peek and Aboo rampaged through the enemy ranks on her right, their massive fists sending soldiers flying like ragdolls. Sarah the medic moved through the battlefield, her luminous wings marking her as a beacon of hope for the wounded.

And somewhere beyond the chaos, Prince William waited. Watching. Waiting for her to come to him.

"LITTLE RAPTOR!" His hundred voices cut through the din of battle. "STOP PLAYING WITH PAWNS! COME FACE YOUR GOD!"

Kira looked up at him, floating above the carnage, wreathed in stolen power. She thought about her mother, who had hidden her wings her entire life. She thought about her father, who had lost his first love to a plague that took the good and left the wicked. She thought about Henry and Owen and even Charles, all of them choosing to stand against impossible odds.

She thought about Peek and Aboo, asking their riddles in that cave so long ago. "What is mightier than the mightiest king, eviler than the devil, and you'll die if you eat it?"

The answer was nothing.

Nothing was mightier than a king who ruled with wisdom. Nothing was eviler than a devil. And if you ate nothing, you would die.

But there was another answer too. One Kira was only now beginning to understand.

The answer was also surrender. Surrender was mightier than any king because it took more courage than fighting. Surrender could defeat evil because it refused to become evil in return. And if you surrendered to the wrong thing, it would destroy you.

But if you surrendered to the right thing, if you surrendered to trust and hope and love, it could save everything.

Kira squeezed Henry's hand one last time as she saw him disappear into the tunnel entrance with Charles. "Together," she whispered, though he could no longer hear her.

"Together," Owen said beside her, as if answering for his brother.

Kira flew toward Prince William, and the final battle began. "For Latavia!" Her cry echoed through tents, camps, and the hills beyond...

Chapter 8: The Dragon Wakes

The earth shook; not the trembling of combat that had raged since dawn, but something deeper. Something that had been building since the blood moon rose five days ago. Every drop of blood spilled in anger, every transformation witnessed, every choice made between violence and peace… all of it had been pressing down on the ancient being sleeping below, until finally, inevitably, it could sleep no more.

Kira flew around Prince William, her wings beating hard to keep her steady as the ground beneath the battlefield began to crack. Soldiers from both armies stumbled and fell. Horses screamed and reared. Even the devolved creatures stopped their mindless charges, some primal instinct warning them of danger beyond their understanding.

"What is that?" Owen shouted from somewhere below.

Kira knew. This tremor throbbed through her once before, years ago, when she and Henry had stood at the edge of the Forbidden Lands and the earth had whispered secrets to those who could hear. The tree sisters had told her about the ancient ones who slept beneath the world. The beings who had existed before kingdoms, before humans, before even the blood moon began its hundred-year cycle.

The dragon was waking.

Prince William felt it too. His stolen powers flickered unstably beneath his skin, the phoenix fire warring with basilisk ice, both of them reacting to something older and stronger than either. His face twisted with something that might have been fear if he were still human enough to feel it.

"No," he snarled, and a hundred voices echoed from his throat. "Not yet. I am not ready. I have not consumed enough power."

The ground split open.

Not at the ruined shrine where they had collapsed the stairs days ago. That entrance remained buried under tons of rubble, sealed by Peek and Aboo's desperate work. This fissure opened at the center of the battlefield, exactly where Kira had been planning to land. Exactly where two armies had been killing each other moments before.

Soldiers scrambled away from the widening crack. Steam rose from the depths, carrying with it the smell of ancient fire and older magic. The blood moon's light seemed to bend toward the opening, as if drawn by something more powerful than the moon itself.

A claw emerged.

It was bronze and gold and copper, scales gleaming with inner fire, each talon longer than a man was tall. The claw gripped the edge of the fissure and pulled, and more of the creature followed. A leg. A shoulder. A wing that unfurled like a storm cloud made solid, blocking out half the sky.

The dragon rose. Kira had seen dragons before. Small ones, caged in Prince William's dungeons during that terrible visit to Romaland. She had helped free a young dragon during the feast of horrors, had watched it breathe fire at the guards who had held it captive. She had thought she understood what dragons were.

She had understood nothing.

This dragon was to those captive creatures what the ocean was to a puddle. What the sun was to a candle. What the blood moon was to a torch. It rose from the earth like a mountain deciding to move, and its eyes held the weight of millennia.

Those eyes were gold flecked with silver, ancient beyond imagining, and they swept across the battlefield with the calm assessment of a being that had watched countless armies rise and fall. They found Prince William hovering in the air, his stolen powers blazing around him like a bonfire. They found Kira with her spread wings and her raptor heritage. They found Henry and Owen and Charles on the ground, frozen in their interrupted combat.

They found Peek and Aboo, still wearing their shared tunic with both kingdoms' colors stitched together.

The dragon spoke.

"WHO DARES DISTURB MY SLUMBER?"

The voice was not sound. It was vibration. It was meaning pressed directly into the mind, bypassing ears entirely. The words pulsed through her bones, in her blood, in the ancient raptor instincts that told her to flee from a predator she could never defeat.

Prince William did not flee. He flew higher, positioning himself level with the dragon's enormous head, and his smile was the smile of a madman who had finally found his ultimate prize.

"I dare," he said, and his hundred stolen voices rang with triumph. "I am Prince William of Romaland. I have consumed the essence of creatures beyond counting. I have absorbed the power of phoenix and basilisk and unicorn. And now I will consume you."

The dragon's laugh shook the foundations of the world.

"CONSUME ME?" The ancient eyes focused on William with something that might have been amusement. "LITTLE THIEF. LITTLE HUNGER WITH HUMAN SKIN. I AM NOT POWER TO BE CONSUMED. I AM JUDGMENT TO BE RENDERED."

William attacked.

Phoenix fire blazed from his hands, hot enough to melt stone. Basilisk venom dripped from claws that had grown where fingers used to be. The stolen essence of fifty devoured creatures poured out of him in a torrent of borrowed power, all of it directed at the dragon's heart.

The dragon did not move.

The fire splashed against ancient scales and dissipated like morning mist. The venom sizzled and evaporated before it could touch bronze flesh. The borrowed powers, stolen from creatures who had screamed as

William consumed them, simply ceased to be when they encountered something older than stealing itself.

"I SEE WHAT YOU ARE," the dragon said, and its voice was almost gentle. Almost sad. "I SEE EVERY SOUL YOU HAVE DEVOURED. THEY CRY OUT FROM WITHIN YOU, BEGGING FOR RELEASE. THE PHOENIX WHO WANTED ONLY TO FLY FREE. THE BASILISK WHO GUARDED ITS EGGS. THE UNICORN WHO HEALED THE SICK."

William screamed and threw more power at the dragon. His body flickered between forms, human and monster and something in between, as if all the creatures he had consumed were trying to escape at once.

"YOU TOOK THEM," the dragon continued. "YOU UNMADE THEM. YOU MADE THEIR ESSENCE YOURS. BUT ESSENCE STOLEN IS ESSENCE CORRUPTED. POWER DEVOURED IS POWER POISONED. YOU HAVE MADE YOURSELF STRONG, LITTLE THIEF. BUT YOU HAVE ALSO MADE YOURSELF A PRISON."

Kira watched from a distance, afraid to move, afraid to draw the dragon's attention. Around her, both armies had frozen. Latavian and Romalander, transformed and unchanged, all of them united in their terror of the ancient being that had risen from the earth.

Henry appeared at her side. She had not seen him approach, but suddenly he was there, his sword still drawn but his eyes fixed on the dragon.

"What do we do?" he asked.

"I do not know." Kira's voice was barely a whisper. "I have never seen anything like this. Even the tree sisters, even Francis and Ida and Mabel, they spoke of dragons as legends. Things that existed long ago, before the forests learned to speak."

"It is not attacking us," Henry observed. "It attacked William because William attacked first. But it is not hurting anyone else."

He was right. The dragon's fire had not spread beyond William's immediate vicinity. Its claws had not slashed at the soldiers who cowered nearby. Its wings, wider than the entire battlefield, had settled against its back as if it had no intention of using them for violence.

"I SEE ALL OF YOU."

The dragon's voice swept across the battlefield, touching every mind. The voice entered her consciousness, read her thoughts, her memories, her deepest fears and hopes. It delighted at choice she had made to reveal her wings. The friends she had defended. The enemies she had spared.

"THE BLOOD MOON HAS JUDGED YOU," the dragon continued. "IT HAS REVEALED YOUR TRUE NATURES. THE CRUEL HAVE BECOME BEASTS. THE KIND HAVE BECOME ANGELS. THE

GREEDY HAVE GROWN GOLDEN CLAWS THAT WILL NEVER HOLD LOVE. THE LIARS HAVE LOST THEIR TONGUES."

The dragon's eyes swept across the battlefield again, seeing everything, judging everything.

"BUT JUDGMENT IS NOT PUNISHMENT. JUDGMENT IS TRUTH. WHAT YOU DO WITH THAT TRUTH IS YOUR OWN CHOICE."

Silver-gold fire erupted from the dragon's maw.

But this was not the destructive fire of combat. This fire was light and warmth and something almost like love. It washed across the battlefield in a gentle wave, touching every soldier, every creature, every being who had gathered for war.

It floated over her, and instead of burning, it asked a question.

Violence or peace?

She thought about her mother, who had hidden her wings to protect her family. She thought about the tree sisters, who had chosen to trust humans after centuries of hatred. She thought about Peek and Aboo, who had evolved from monsters to friends through the simple act of choosing laughter over cruelty.

Peace, she answered. I choose peace.

The fire passed through her and moved on. Around her, she saw soldiers making the same choice. Transformed and unchanged, Latavian and Romalander, all of them confronted with the same question. All of them given the same opportunity to decide what kind of beings they wanted to be.

Most chose peace. Not all. Some soldiers, their hearts too hardened by years of hatred, chose violence. They screamed as the dragon's fire burned hotter around them, not destroying but transforming, accelerating the blood moon's judgment until they became fully the beasts they had always been inside.

But most chose peace. Most laid down their weapons. Most walked toward the center of the battlefield, toward the dragon's light, toward each other.

Only Prince William remained untouched by the choice. The fire could not reach him. The judgment could not penetrate the layers of stolen power that armored his soul. He hovered in the air, screaming defiance, throwing attack after attack at an enemy who simply ignored him.

"YOU CANNOT JUDGE ME!" he shrieked. "I AM BEYOND JUDGMENT! I HAVE CONSUMED TOO MUCH POWER! I AM BECOME A GOD!"

The dragon turned its ancient eyes toward him one last time.

"YOU ARE BECOME A PRISON," it said sadly. "AND THE PRISONERS ARE SCREAMING TO BE FREE."

The dragon settled to the ground, its massive body crushing the earth beneath it. The fissure from which it had emerged began to close, the world healing itself around the ancient being's presence. The blood moon hung overhead, watching, waiting, its seven-day judgment nearly complete.

"THE CHOICE IS BEFORE YOU," the dragon announced to the gathered armies. "YOU HAVE SEEN WHAT VIOLENCE BRINGS. YOU HAVE SEEN WHAT PEACE OFFERS. THE BLOOD MOON SETS TOMORROW. WHAT YOU CHOOSE BETWEEN NOW AND THEN WILL DETERMINE WHETHER YOUR KINGDOMS SURVIVE ANOTHER HUNDRED YEARS."

It turned its head toward Kira, and the attention focused on her was like the weight of mountains.

"RAPTOR PRINCESS. YOU HAVE ALREADY CHOSEN. YOU REVEALED YOUR TRUE SELF WHEN HIDING WOULD HAVE BEEN SAFER. YOU STOOD FOR THOSE WHO COULD NOT STAND FOR THEMSELVES. YOU EARNED THE LOYALTY OF TROLLS AND FROGS AND FORMER ENEMIES."

Kira could not speak. Could not move. Could only listen as judgment was rendered upon her.

"YOUR MOTHER MADE THE SAME CHOICE, LONG AGO. SHE HID HER WINGS TO PROTECT HER CHILD, BUT SHE NEVER HID HER HEART. WHEN THE PLAGUE CAME, SHE

STAYED TO HELP THE SICK INSTEAD OF FLEEING TO SAFETY. SHE CHOSE LOVE OVER SURVIVAL."

Tears ran down Kira's face. She had not known. Had not understood why her mother had stayed, had died, had left her daughter alone with only questions and grief.

"YOU KILLED NO ONE WITH THAT CHOICE," the dragon said gently. "THE PLAGUE KILLED HER. HER LOVE KEPT HER THERE. YOU WERE NOT THE CAUSE. YOU WERE THE REASON."

The dragon's wing extended, a gesture almost like a blessing.

"GO NOW, RAPTOR PRINCESS. THE THIEF MUST FACE HIS OWN JUDGMENT. THE PRISONERS WITHIN HIM MUST BE FREED. BUT THAT IS NOT YOUR BATTLE. YOUR BATTLE IS CONVINCING YOUR PEOPLE THAT PEACE IS POSSIBLE. THAT EVOLUTION IS A GIFT. THAT THE BLOOD MOON'S JUDGMENT IS NOT A CURSE BUT AN OPPORTUNITY."

Kira found her voice. "How? How do I convince them of something I am not certain I believe myself?"

"YOU HAVE ALREADY BEGUN." The dragon's eyes held something that might have been warmth. "LOOK AROUND YOU. LOOK AT WHAT YOUR CHOICE HAS INSPIRED."

She looked.

She saw Owen standing beside Henry, brothers reunited across the lines of war. She saw Charles kneeling, not in defeat but in acknowledgment of his mistakes. She saw Peek and Aboo helping a wounded Romalander soldier to his feet, their massive hands gentle despite their strength.

She saw transformed and unchanged standing together. Latavian and Romalander no longer separated by fear. The devolved creatures huddled at the edges, uncertain what they had become, but no longer attacking. The evolved soldiers, those who had grown wings or scales or stranger things, no longer hiding in shame.

"They stopped fighting," she whispered.

"THEY MADE A CHOICE," the dragon corrected. "THE SAME CHOICE YOU MADE. THE SAME CHOICE YOUR MOTHER MADE. THE SAME CHOICE EVERY BEING MUST MAKE WHEN JUDGMENT COMES."

The dragon's head turned toward Prince William, who still hovered above the battlefield, still screaming, still throwing useless attacks.

"NOW. THERE IS ONE MORE CHOICE TO BE MADE. AND IT IS NOT YOURS TO MAKE."

Chapter 9: The Choice

Day Six - The Final Sunrise

Dawn broke over the battlefield. Kira hovered three hundred feet above the armies, her wings beating against air thick with the blood moon's fading magic...

Below her, two armies had stopped fighting. Behind her, an ancient dragon waited with the patience of millennia. Before her, Prince William blazed with stolen power, barely recognizable as human anymore.

This was the moment from the prologue. The moment she had seen in her mind when the blood moon first rose. The moment everything had been building toward.

"I have become a god, little raptor," William said, and his words distorted reality around them. "I have eaten the strength of fifty soldiers, the magic of a dozen creatures, the very essence of power itself. Your wings are beautiful, but they are just meat. And I am so very hungry."

He moved faster than physics should allow, crossing the distance between them in a blink. His hand, now tipped with claws that should not exist on human fingers, slashed toward her throat.

Kira twisted in mid-air, her raptor instincts screaming warnings a heartbeat before his attack. The claws found her neck, tearing a line that spilled a trickle of blood. She countered with her sword, but William caught the blade with his bare palm.

The metal sizzled against his phoenix-enhanced flesh, and he laughed.

"You cannot hurt me," he said, crushing her sword to fragments with a grip that leaked stolen power like light through cracks. "I regenerate. I adapt. I consume."

He was right. Nothing she had could defeat him. Not her sword, now broken. Not her training, useless against his speed. Not her wings, which only gave her more ways to dodge attacks she could never return.

Below, she saw Henry fighting Stanislas in a desperate ground battle. Owen tried to reach them but was blocked by the last of William's loyal guards. Charles held his position near the wounded, protecting them from any stray attacks. Peek and Aboo formed a living wall between the devolved creatures and the soldiers who had chosen peace.

Everyone was fighting. Everyone except the dragon, who watched with ancient eyes, waiting for something only it could see.

William lunged again, and this time his claws found her arm. Pain blazed through her as phoenix fire burned the wound even as basilisk venom tried to paralyze her muscles. She fell, spiraling toward the ground, barely catching herself before she crashed.

"That is one," William gloated, floating down toward her. "Soon I will have both your wings. And then I will have your essence. And then, perhaps, I will finally be strong enough to consume the dragon itself."

Kira landed hard, one wing dragging uselessly, her arm bleeding and burning. She looked up at the monster William had become and saw no path to victory. He was too fast. Too strong. Too armored in stolen power.

She could not win this fight.

Henry saw Kira fall.

He screamed her name and tried to break away from Stanislas, but his half-brother was too skilled, too determined, too willing to die to prevent Henry from reaching the princess. Their swords clashed again and again, neither able to gain advantage.

"Give up," Stanislas snarled between strikes. "Your princess is finished. Your kingdom is finished. Everything you love will be consumed."

"I will never give up," Henry shot back. "Owen believed in me. The trolls believed in me. Kira believed in me when I was just a Romalander slave with nothing but a wooden horse. I will not abandon her now."

"Owen is a fool," Stanislas said, but something flickered in his eyes. Pain. Regret. The echo of a brotherhood that might have been different if circumstances had been different. "We could have ruled together. The three of us. Brothers united. Instead, you chose them over your own blood."

"I chose family," Henry answered. "Real family. The kind you earn, not the kind you are born into. The kind that stands with you when the darkness comes."

He saw Kira struggling to rise, saw William closing in for the final attack. Saw the dragon waiting, watching, judging.

And he understood.

The dragon had said the choice was not Kira's to make. But it was not William's choice either. The choice belonged to everyone. The choice was whether to fight or to surrender. Whether to keep trying to win through violence or to trust that peace was possible.

Kira had made her choice three days ago when she revealed her wings. She had surrendered her secret, trusted her people with the truth, and in doing so had transformed the nature of the conflict entirely. Now it was time for everyone else to choose.

Kira watched William descend toward her. His claws extended. His stolen powers blazed. His hundred devoured voices whispered hunger and triumph.

She could not defeat him. But maybe she did not need to. She thought about the riddle of the twin trolls, two years ago in that cave. *"If you can only bring one thing into battle, what would it be?"* Henry had answered a sword. But Kira had known better even then, hadn't she? The answer was nothing. A wise ruler does not need the sword. And if her mother could face plague without a weapon, if Queen Kirena could choose love over survival, then perhaps Kira could choose trust over violence. Perhaps that was what evolution truly meant—not growing wings, but growing brave enough to put them down. "If you can only bring one thing into battle, what would it be?" Henry had answered a sword. But Kira had known the real answer.

Nothing.

A wise ruler does not need the sword. Sometimes, the bravest thing a warrior can do is choose to lose.

Kira threw away her broken sword.

William paused, confused by the gesture. Enemies did not disarm themselves. Prey did not stop running. This was not how the hunt was supposed to end.

Kira spread her wings, making herself completely vulnerable.

"Henry," she called, her voice carrying across the battlefield with a strength that surprised even her. "Now."

And Henry, because he had always understood her even when she did not understand herself, saw what she was doing. He saw that sometimes the bravest thing a warrior could do was choose to lose. He threw down his own blade mid-strike, leaving himself defenseless before Stanislas's descending sword.

Stanislas's sword stopped an inch from Henry's throat.

"What are you doing?" he demanded. "Fight me. Die with honor if you must die."

"No," Henry said calmly. "I am done fighting. The war is over."

Charles saw them both surrender. Saw the princess he had betrayed and the squire he had trained, choosing peace over victory. And in that moment, the old knight who had spent his whole life proving his worth through strength finally understood:

True strength was knowing when to stop fighting.

Charles dropped his sword.

The clatter of steel on stone echoed across the silent battlefield. One sword. Then another. Then a dozen. Then a hundred.

Soldiers on both sides watched their champions disarm themselves. Watched the most skilled warriors in two kingdoms lay down their weapons and choose vulnerability over violence. And one by one, following their example, they made the same choice.

Swords fell to the grass like rain. Owen reached his brothers in the sudden silence.

Stanislas still held his sword, the blade trembling inches from Henry's throat. His face was a war of emotions. Anger. Confusion. Something that might have been hope if he remembered how to feel it.

"Put it down," Owen said quietly. "Please, brother. We can end this. All of us. Together."

"I cannot," Stanislas whispered. "If I surrender, William will kill me. If I fight, you will kill me. There is no path where I survive."

"There is," Henry said, not moving, not threatening, just speaking the truth. "You can choose differently. Right now. Right here. You can be the brother we lost. The brother we want to find again."

"It is too late for me."

"It is never too late." Owen stepped closer, his own sword long since dropped. "The blood moon judges what we are. But we choose what we become. Charles chose to betray us, and then he chose to help us. Kira chose to hide her wings, and then she chose to reveal them. The transformed soldiers chose cruelty, and some of them devolved. Others chose kindness, and they evolved."

He held out his hand.

"Choose, Stanislas. Not what you were. What you want to be."

The moment stretched. The blood moon hung overhead, watching. The dragon waited with ancient patience. Two armies held their breath.

Stanislas's sword fell.

He took Owen's hand.

And the last of the fighting ended.

Prince William screamed. It was a scream of pain, a scream of anger.

He stood alone now, hovering above a battlefield where everyone had chosen peace. His loyal soldiers had surrendered. His brother had betrayed him. His enemies had refused to fight.

"This is not how it ends," he raged, stolen power crackling around him like a storm. "I am the most powerful being in existence. I have consumed gods and monsters. You cannot defeat me by putting down your weapons."

Kira walked toward him.

Her wings spread behind her, tattered and bleeding but still beautiful. Her arm hung useless at her side, poison and fire still warring in the wound. She was injured and exhausted and utterly defenseless.

But she was not afraid.

"You are right," she said calmly. "We cannot defeat you. We are not trying to defeat you."

"Then what are you doing?"

"Showing you something." She gestured at the armies that surrounded him, at the soldiers who had chosen to stop fighting, at the brothers reunited and the enemies reconciled and the transformed and unchanged standing together. "This is what peace looks like. This is what surrender means. Not weakness. Not defeat. Just the courage to stop hurting each other."

"That is not courage," William snarled. "That is cowardice."

"Then why are you the only one still afraid?"

He recoiled as if she had struck him.

"I am not afraid," he said, but his voice wavered. "I am never afraid. I have consumed enough power to destroy everything. Everyone. I could kill you all right now. I could burn your armies. I could level your kingdoms. I could feast on your bones and add your essence to my own."

"Then do it."

Kira spread her arms, making herself an even easier target.

"We are not fighting back. We are not running. We are just standing here, choosing peace. If you want to kill us, there is nothing stopping you."

William's claws flexed. His stolen powers surged. A hundred consumed voices screamed for blood.

But he did not attack.

"Why?" Kira asked softly. "Why can you not do it? Why can you not kill people who are not fighting back?"

"Because..." He hesitated, and for a moment, something human flickered in his eyes. "Because that is not... it is not..."

"Not what?"

"Not victory," he whispered. "Killing the defenseless is not victory. It is just... slaughter."

"Yes," Kira said. "It is. And somewhere deep inside all that stolen power, you still know the difference."

The dragon spoke.

"INTERESTING," it rumbled, and its ancient voice held something like respect. "I HAVE WATCHED HUMANS FOR MILLENNIA. I

HAVE SEEN THEM CHOOSE VIOLENCE OVER AND OVER. WARS WITHOUT END. HATRED WITHOUT LIMIT. BUT THIS... THIS I HAVE NEVER SEEN."

Its enormous head swung toward Kira.

"YOU CHOSE PEACE WHEN FIGHTING WOULD HAVE BEEN EASIER. YOU SURRENDERED WHEN VICTORY WAS STILL POSSIBLE. AND IN DOING SO, YOU CHANGED THE NATURE OF THE BATTLE ITSELF."

"I did not change anything," Kira said. "Everyone made their own choice."

"YES. BUT YOU SHOWED THEM THAT ANOTHER CHOICE WAS POSSIBLE. THAT IS LEADERSHIP. THAT IS EVOLUTION. THAT IS WHAT THE BLOOD MOON HOPES TO FIND EVERY HUNDRED YEARS."

The dragon turned its attention to William.

"AND YOU, LITTLE THIEF. YOU HAVE CONSUMED POWER BEYOND IMAGINING. YOU HAVE MADE YOURSELF A PRISON FOR STOLEN SOULS. BUT EVEN NOW, EVEN AT THE END, YOU CANNOT KILL THE DEFENSELESS. THERE IS STILL SOMETHING HUMAN IN YOU. SOMETHING WORTH SAVING."

"I do not want to be saved," William snarled.

"NO. YOU WANT TO BE A GOD. BUT GODS DO NOT CONSUME. GODS CREATE. GODS PROTECT. GODS SERVE

SOMETHING LARGER THAN THEMSELVES." The dragon's eyes held no anger, only ancient sadness. "KNEEL, LITTLE THIEF. KNEEL AND I WILL RELEASE THE SOULS YOU HAVE IMPRISONED. KNEEL AND I WILL GIVE YOU ANOTHER CHANCE TO BE HUMAN."

"And if I refuse?"

"THEN YOU REMAIN A PRISON. FOREVER. THE SOULS YOU HAVE CONSUMED WILL SCREAM WITHIN YOU FOR ETERNITY. YOU WILL NEVER KNOW PEACE. NEVER KNOW REST. NEVER KNOW ANYTHING BUT HUNGER AND THE MEMORY OF WHAT YOU DESTROYED."

William looked at the armies that had chosen peace. At the brothers who had reunited. At the princess who had surrendered and somehow won.

He looked at what he had become. What he had lost. What he could never get back if he chose to remain a monster.

"I cannot kneel," he said finally. "I have consumed too much. The power will not let me."

"THE POWER IS NOT YOU," the dragon said. "YOU ARE STILL SOMEWHERE INSIDE. FIND YOURSELF. CHOOSE YOURSELF. AND KNEEL."

Prince William, the terror of two kingdoms, the consumer of souls, the would-be god... fell to his knees.

Chapter 10: Evolution

The dragon breathed judgment. Not the silver-gold fire of choice that had washed over the armies earlier. This was something deeper. Something that reached into William's stolen essence and found every soul he had consumed, every power he had devoured, every life he had unmade to feed his endless hunger.

William screamed.

But it was not a scream of pain. It was a scream of release. The stolen powers erupted from him like prisoners breaking free from chains. Phoenix fire spiraled into the sky, forming briefly into the shape of a great bird before dissipating into dawn light. Basilisk venom turned to mist and faded. Unicorn grace became a shimmer of silver that blessed everyone it touched before vanishing.

Soul after soul emerged from William's collapsing form. The soldiers he had consumed. The creatures he had devoured. The innocents he had unmade. Each one briefly visible, briefly themselves again, before passing on to whatever waited beyond.

"Thank you," one whispered as it passed Kira. "Thank you for ending it."

She had not ended it. The dragon had. William himself had, in the final moment, when he chose to kneel instead of remain a monster. But she nodded anyway, accepting the gratitude, honoring the freed souls with her witness.

When it was over, Prince William lay on the grass. Not hovering. Not burning with stolen power. Just a man. Pale and thin and shaking, his eyes brown again, only brown, with no flicker of other colors.

The sixth day was ending. Tomorrow, the blood moon would set, and the judgment would be complete.

He looked up at the dragon with something that might have been wonder if he remembered how to feel it.

"What did you do to me?"

"I RETURNED YOU TO YOURSELF," the dragon said. "THE POWER IS GONE. THE SOULS ARE FREE. YOU ARE SIMPLY WILLIAM AGAIN."

"I do not remember how to be simply William."

"THEN LEARN." The dragon's voice was not unkind. "YOU HAVE COMMITTED TERRIBLE CRIMES. YOU HAVE CONSUMED INNOCENT SOULS. BUT YOU ALSO KNELT WHEN KNEELING WAS THE HARDEST THING YOU COULD DO. THAT COUNTS FOR SOMETHING."

"What happens now?"

"NOW YOU FACE THE CONSEQUENCES OF YOUR CHOICES. NOT FROM ME. FROM THE PEOPLE YOU HURT. THE

KINGDOMS YOU TERRORIZED. THE SURVIVORS WHO MUST DECIDE WHETHER TO OFFER MERCY OR DEMAND JUSTICE."

The dragon turned its ancient eyes to the assembled armies.

"THAT IS YOUR TASK NOW. ALL OF YOU. THE BLOOD MOON SETS. THE JUDGMENT IS COMPLETE. WHAT YOU BUILD FROM THIS MOMENT FORWARD IS YOUR OWN RESPONSIBILITY."

Day Seven - Final Dawn

The blood moon set as the sun rose. Kira watched the crimson light fade from the sky, replaced by ordinary gold, ordinary warmth. The world looked different in daylight. Clearer somehow. More honest.

She looked down at her wings. They were still there. Tattered and wounded from the battle, but still part of her. The blood moon had revealed them, but it had not given them to her. They had always been hers. She had just been too afraid to claim them.

"They are not changing back," she said quietly.

"No," the dragon confirmed. "THE BLOOD MOON REVEALS. IT DOES NOT RESTORE. WHAT YOU HAVE BECOME IS WHAT YOU NOW ARE."

Around the battlefield, transformed soldiers were making the same discovery. Those who had evolved, whose kindness had given them wings or healing hands or other gifts, found that the gifts remained. Those who had devolved, whose cruelty had made them beasts, found that the beast was now their permanent form.

"It is permanent," someone cried. "We are stuck like this forever."

"YOU ARE NOT STUCK," the dragon corrected. "YOU ARE REVEALED. THE BLOOD MOON SHOWED YOUR TRUE NATURE. SOME OF YOU WERE KIND BENEATH YOUR MASKS. SOME WERE CRUEL. NONE OF YOU CAN HIDE ANYMORE."

"But that is not fair," another voice protested. "I made mistakes. I was cruel sometimes. But I was learning. I was trying to be better."

"THEN CONTINUE LEARNING. CONTINUE TRYING." The dragon's gaze swept across the crowd. "EVOLUTION IS NOT A DESTINATION. IT IS A JOURNEY. THE BLOOD MOON JUDGED WHAT YOU WERE AT THIS MOMENT. WHAT YOU BECOME TOMORROW IS STILL YOUR CHOICE."

Henry stepped forward, his hand still clasped with Owen's. Stanislas stood behind them, uncertain, but present.

"What about those who chose peace?" Henry asked. "Those who surrendered? Does that count for something?"

"IT COUNTS FOR EVERYTHING." The dragon's voice held warmth now. "YOU SHOWED THAT HUMANS CAN CHOOSE DIFFERENTLY. THAT VIOLENCE IS NOT INEVITABLE. THAT ENEMIES CAN BECOME BROTHERS AND KINGDOMS CAN

BECOME ALLIES. THAT IS THE EVOLUTION THE BLOOD MOON HOPED TO FIND."

"And you?" Kira asked. "What happens to you now?"

"I RETURN TO SLUMBER. I HAVE WALKED THIS WORLD FOR MILLENNIA, AND I AM TIRED. BUT I WILL DREAM, AND IN MY DREAMS I WILL WATCH. I WILL SEE WHAT YOU BUILD. WHAT YOU BECOME. WHETHER THE PEACE YOU CHOSE TODAY BECOMES THE PEACE YOU MAINTAIN TOMORROW."

The dragon began to sink back into the earth. The fissure opened again beneath it, swallowing the ancient being like the world itself drawing a long breath.

"REMEMBER," it said as it descended. "THE BLOOD MOON WILL RETURN IN ANOTHER HUNDRED YEARS. IT WILL JUDGE YOUR DESCENDANTS AS IT JUDGED YOU. TEACH THEM WELL. SHOW THEM THAT EVOLUTION IS POSSIBLE. THAT PEACE IS A CHOICE. THAT WHAT YOU ARE MATTERS LESS THAN WHAT YOU CHOOSE TO BECOME."

The fissure closed.

The dragon was gone.

And two armies stood in the light of a new day, wondering what to do next.

King Phillip found Kira at the edge of the battlefield. The blood moon had set hours ago. She was sitting on a fallen log, her wounded wing wrapped in bandages that Sarah the medic had applied. Her arm was in a sling, the phoenix burn and basilisk venom slowly healing under the evolved woman's care. She looked exhausted but alive.

More importantly, she looked at peace.

"You did it," the king said, sitting beside her. "You ended the war."

"I did not end anything." Kira shook her head. "Everyone chose to end it together. I just... showed them it was possible."

"That is what leaders do." King Phillip put his arm around her, careful of her injuries. "They show what is possible. They go first into the darkness so others can follow into the light."

"I was terrified."

"I know. I was watching. I saw you throw away your sword. Saw you spread your wings and make yourself a target. I thought I was going to lose you." His voice cracked slightly. "I thought I was going to lose my daughter the same way I lost her mother."

Kira leaned against him, feeling his warmth, his strength, his love.

"The dragon said something," she told him. "About mother. About why she stayed during the plague. It said I did not kill her. The plague killed her. Her love kept her there."

"It was right," King Phillip said quietly. "I have always known that. I hoped someday you would know it too."

"I think I am starting to understand." Kira looked at her wings, at the bandages, at the scars that would mark her forever. "She hid her wings to protect me. But she never hid her heart. And in the end, her heart is what mattered."

"Just like yours."

They sat together in the morning light, father and daughter, king and princess, ordinary and extraordinary all at once.

The work of rebuilding took weeks.

The Romalanders went home, but not as enemies. Owen stayed to help coordinate, serving as ambassador between the two kingdoms. Stanislas went with the Romalander forces, but as a prisoner of his own people, facing trial for his crimes. Henry accompanied him partway, the two brothers speaking words that had gone unspoken for too long.

Prince William was taken to Latavia in chains. Not to be executed. Kira had argued against that, had reminded the council of the dragon's words. He had knelt. He had chosen, in the final moment, to be human again. That had to count for something.

Instead, he would spend his life making amends. Rebuilding what he had destroyed. Serving the people he had terrorized. Learning what it meant to be simply William, without power, without hunger, without the ability to consume anyone ever again.

Charles faced his own trial. The charges were serious. Treason. Kidnapping. Sabotage. But Kira spoke for him, reminded the judges of his final choice, of the warning he had brought, of the sword he had laid down when laying it down was the hardest thing he could do.

He was exiled. Not executed, not imprisoned, but sent away from the kingdom he had served for twenty years. Sent to start over somewhere else, to prove that evolution was possible even for those who had fallen furthest.

"I will make you proud," he told Kira as he left. "Someday. Somehow. I will earn back what I threw away."

"You cannot earn back trust," she told him. "But you can build new trust. Different trust. That is what evolution means."

The transformed soldiers integrated slowly into both kingdoms. Some found their new abilities useful. Sarah the medic became the most famous healer in Latavia, her luminous wings marking her as someone who had chosen kindness even before the blood moon made it visible. Others struggled with bodies that no longer matched their memories of themselves.

The devolved creatures were harder. Some could not be reached, had become too beast-like to remember being human. They were released into the Forbidden Lands, where the tree sisters agreed to watch over them. Others retained enough humanity to learn new ways of living, to find purpose even in forms they had not chosen.

Peek and Aboo became heroes. Songs were sung about the twin trolls who had stood against an army, who had worn both kingdoms' colors, who had helped hold the line when everything seemed lost. They were embarrassed by the attention but secretly pleased.

"We just did what friends do," Peek said when someone asked about their bravery.

"Friends protect friends," Aboo agreed. "Even when friends are being stupid."

"Especially when friends are being stupid," Peek corrected.

On the last day of the peace ceremonies, three weeks after the blood moon had set, Kira and Henry stood at the edge of the battlefield where everything had changed.

The fissure had sealed completely, no trace remaining of the dragon's emergence. Grass was already growing over the scars of combat. In a few years, there would be no physical evidence that two armies had nearly destroyed each other here.

But the memory would remain. Passed down through stories and songs. Taught to children who would teach their own children. The day the war ended because a princess threw away her sword.

"What happens now?" Henry asked.

"We rebuild," Kira said. "We teach. We show people that what the blood moon revealed is not a curse but a gift. We prove that evolution is possible not just during the seven days, but every day after."

"That sounds like a lot of work."

"It is." She smiled at him, her oldest friend, her most trusted companion. "But we have faced complicated before. We survived the Forbidden Lands. We survived the tree sisters. We survived the feast of horrors. We survived a prince who wanted to eat our souls."

"We survived together," Henry said.

"Always together."

She spread her wings, wincing slightly at the pull of healing muscles. The sun caught the feathers, making them shimmer with colors that had no name.

"Race you to the castle?"

"That is cheating. You have wings."

"Then I suppose you had better find a fast horse." She grinned at him, the expression carrying echoes of the girl she had been and the woman she was becoming. "Unless you are afraid of losing."

"I am never afraid of losing to you."

"Good answer."

She launched herself into the air, her wings catching the wind, carrying her higher and higher until she was just a silhouette against the morning sun. Below, Henry ran for the stables, already knowing he would lose but not caring.

Some races were not about winning.

Some races were about running together.

And as Kira flew toward the castle, toward her father and her kingdom and the thousand challenges that waited, she felt something she had not experienced in a very long time.

Hope.

Not the desperate hope of someone fighting against impossible odds. Not the fragile hope of someone afraid it would be taken away. Just hope. Simple and strong and real.

The hope of someone who had faced the worst and discovered that the worst could be survived. That enemies could become friends. That monsters could choose to be human. That peace was possible if enough people were brave enough to choose it. The war games were over, but the real work was just beginning.

THE END

An Excerpt from Book 5

Edict of Love

The royal decree arrived at breakfast as Kira was picking at her eggs, still exhausted from weeks of rebuilding after the war games The messenger burst through the dining hall doors. He wore the colors of the High Council, gold and silver thread on black velvet, and his face carried the particular smugness of someone delivering news they knew would cause trouble.

"For Her Royal Highness, Princess Kira of Latavia." He held out the scroll with a flourish. "From the Council of Noble Houses."

King Phillip reached for it, but the messenger pulled back. "Apologies, Your Majesty. The edict is addressed to the princess directly. Council protocol demands she receive it first."

Kira exchanged a glance with Henry, who sat across from her. His fork had frozen halfway to his mouth. They both knew what edicts from the Council usually meant.

Nothing good.

She took the scroll and broke the seal. The wax crumbled beneath her fingers, releasing a faint scent of roses and something sharper beneath. Politics. The smell of politics was always sharper than it should be.

She read the words once. Twice. Three times.

The eggs she had been picking at suddenly looked far less appetizing.

"What does it say?" King Phillip asked.

Kira set the scroll on the table. Her hands were steady. Her voice was not.

"The Council has invoked the Edict of Love."

The words fell into silence. Henry's fork clattered against his plate. King Phillip's face went pale beneath his beard. Even the servants stopped their quiet movements, frozen by words that had not been spoken in Latavia for three generations.

"That is impossible," the king said. "The Edict has not been used since my grandfather's time."

"Apparently, the Council believes these are extraordinary circumstances." Kira picked up the scroll again, reading from it directly. "In light of the recent blood moon transformations, the revelation of the princess's raptor heritage, and the need to strengthen alliances with neighboring kingdoms, the Council of Noble Houses hereby invokes the Edict of Love. Princess Kira of Latavia shall be presented with three suitable marriage candidates within thirty days. She shall choose one within sixty days. The marriage shall take place before the winter solstice."

"They cannot force you to marry," Henry said. His voice was tight. Controlled. The voice of someone holding back a storm.

"They can." Kira set the scroll down again. "The Edict was written into our laws centuries ago. A princess who has revealed magical heritage must marry to prove her bloodline can be trusted. To show that her children will be loyal to Latavia, not to whatever ancient power flows through her veins. She must marry a Latavian."

"That law was written when people feared magic," King Phillip said. "When the blood moon was a curse, not a gift. Surely we can petition to have it overturned."

"The Council anticipated that." Kira pointed to a paragraph near the bottom. "Any petition to overturn the Edict must be approved by a two-thirds majority of the Noble Houses. And the petition process takes a minimum of ninety days."

"Which means the marriage would happen before the petition could be heard," Henry finished. His jaw was clenched so tight Kira could see the muscles jumping beneath his skin.

Kira smiled. Henry had professed his love before, but this was a different kind of feeling she saw spreading through his body. His face, and his hand on his sword. *Did he want to marry her?*

152

The Complete Kira and Henry Series:

- Book 1: Quest into the Forbidden Lands
- Book 2: Lost in the Enchanted Forest
- Book 3: Dangerous Treaty
- Book 4: War Games
- Book 5: Edict of Love
- Book 6: King Kira

About the Author

Sandi Jerome is Sandi is an enrolled and blood member of the Cherokee Nation and a two-time winner of the Native American Media Alliance fellowship. She is a graduate of UCLA's Advanced Screenwriting program. Her screenplay, *Runaway Cricket*, is being produced as an animated musical by BlackOrb.com. She has been a finalist in most of the major contests, Nicholls, Page International and Austin Film Festival.

Sandi grew up on an avocado farm in Escondido and was the "go to" kid to climb up high and pick the top fruit. She would then jump down into the thick pile of leaves and thought she could fly! She created this young adult fantasy series, *Kira and Henry*, where the teen princess must hide the secret that she can fly or be banished from the kingdom. The first book, Kira and Henry: *Quest into the Forbidden Lands*, was a 2nd Rounder in 2023 Austin Film Festival and a 2024 Kindle Book Review finalist.

In her first Native American fellowship, she wrote *Technically Soccer*, a half-hour comedy about a Women's Professional Soccer team getting an AI-Robot coach. Sandi is an avid women's soccer fan; she coached and played soccer for over twenty years. *Blood Moon Wolf* (TV Pilot and Feature) was completed as part of her 2nd Native American fellowship, about a wolf who turns into a girl to become a spirit guide. Her middle-grade book, *Sleep Warrior*, about her Cherokee ancestor, was #3 on Coverfly's Red List of Animated Manuscripts. To get her message into schools, she is seeking a more traditional publisher for her Native American Sleep Warrior series.

As a Floridian and a long-time Disney fan, annual passholder, and certified Disney expert, Sandi wrote *Pixie Dust Death* set at Disney World, then created a non-Disney version, *Wilma Wallaby Genius Girl Detective,* set at a theme park she invented, with a web series in production. She is also the author of the *Amazing Animals of Disney's Animal Kingdom.*

Sandi wrote a book adaptation of *Hijacked* for producer Melissa Shevela of Helicopter Productions. Her next book adaptation to film was Jake and Clara based on the book, *Jake & Clara: Scandal, Politics, Hollywood and Murder* by Wall Street Journal bestselling author, ghostwriter, broadcaster, David R. Stokes. Blair Underwood optioned David's previous book. She and

David wrote a book very personal to Sandi, *Churchill's Mum: The Story of Jennie Jerome,* after years of research connecting Sandi's husband, Keith, to the American heiress who was Winston Churchill's mother and Keith's fifth cousin. It presents the premise that Winston's half-American status helped defeat Hitler. She had done almost a dozen "writer for hire" gigs that involved book adaptations or co-writing books with producers who had a great idea.

Sandi was the first editor of *Digital Dealer* Magazine and wrote computer software reviews for major publications and numerous published computer guides. She sold her technology company in 2022 and now writes full-time, at least 10 pages a day. Her next project will be her Super Series, a continuation of her Super Controller books. Books will be; Super Health, Super Love, Super Wealth and Super Life.

For Sandi, "Writing is life!"

Learn more at www.**SandraJerome**.com or leave comments on her publisher's Contact page, www.**SmilingEagle**.com.